Stealing
the Hopi Snake Dance

A Fernando Lopez Santa Fe Mystery

STEALING
THE HOPI SNAKE DANCE

A FERNANDO LOPEZ SANTA FE MYSTERY

INCLUDES
THE HOPI SNAKE DANCE
by
D. H. LAWRENCE, 1924

JAMES C. WILSON

SUNSTONE
PRESS
SANTA FE

Sunstone books may be purchased for educational, business, or sales promotional use. For information please write: Special Markets Department, Sunstone Press, P.O. Box 2321, Santa Fe, New Mexico 87504-2321.
Printed on acid-free paper
♾
eBook: 978-1-61139-767-3

LIBRARY OF CONGRESS CATALOGING IN PUBLICATION DATA
(ON FILE)

WWW.SUNSTONEPRESS.COM
SUNSTONE PRESS / POST OFFICE BOX 2321 / SANTA FE, NM 87504-2321 /USA
(505) 988-4418

"The Hopi smooths the rattlesnake and carries him in his mouth, to send him back into the dark places of the earth, an emissary to the inner powers."

--D.H. Lawrence, "The Hopi Snake Dance"

THE SNAKE DANCE

Jeff Walker had been waiting for hours, like everyone else in the dusty plaza and on the rooftops of the mud adobes. Waiting for the Snake Dance to begin. Officially the dance was off limits to outsiders, but he'd worn a wide-brimmed straw hat and glasses to disguise himself, plus given a fifty dollar tip to the Hopi directing parking at the bottom of First Mesa. From there he walked up the curving road to Walpi, the Hopi village at the southeast corner of First Mesa where the Snake Dance would be performed this year. The dance was held every other year to promote rain in the arid Hopi homeland, where rain was as scarce as money.

Since arriving he'd suffered through a series of preliminary dances, with the singers chanting and beating on drums over by the kiva. His back ached and his legs were cramping, but he desperately needed the money. Max Russo and his Santa Fe Film Collective had offered him a flat ten thousand dollars to surreptitiously videotape the secretive Hopi Snake Dance. That seemed like a lot of money for a day's work, but Max said he could make a small fortune on a video of the mysterious Hopi Snake Dance. The only authenticated video of the official Snake Dance dated from August 20, 1913, when Teddy Roosevelt was in attendance. Go figure.

Cameras, like outsiders, were banned from the dance, so the problem had been how to conceal his camera. Max had come to him because he had experience with surreptitious recordings, working occasionally for a Santa Fe lawyer on acrimonious divorce cases. This was different, though. He had to stand in front of the crowd and at all times maintain a clear line of sight to the dancers as they moved about the Plaza. In comparison, the concealment problem proved easy. He brought two cameras to make sure he caught the dance. The first was the camera on his iphone 16 Pro, which fit perfectly in his shirt pocket, with the lens exposed and pointing straight ahead. The second was a small round SpyFocus camera tucked inside his western hat. The camera fit just inside the brim of the straw hat, with its round lens protruding through the straw and the pressed tin star affixed to the outside of the hat. The small black lens looked like a precious black stone in the center of the star.

Suddenly Jeff noticed activity at the back of the Plaza. The Snake Dancers were emerging from the kiva one at a time, their faces and naked upper bodies covered with gray and charcoal paint, with white streaks on their arms and a dab of pink on their foreheads. Feathers attached to their leather breeches bobbed and weaved as the painted figures began to dance. Then the singers began beating their drums and chanting: "Ay-ya! Ay-ya! Ay-ya! Ay-ya!"

Now or never! Jeff removed his hat and pretended to wipe his brow with a kerchief while hitting the start button on the SpyFocus camera. He placed the hat back on his head and then took out the iphone from his shirt pocket to ostensibly check for email or whatever. He tapped the start button and then gingerly inserted the iphone in his shirt pocket.

While the drums pounded, the dancers approached the covey hole near the kiva where the snakes were kept and washed clean. "Ay-ya! Ay-ya!" the singers chanted, as the dancers one by one picked up the snakes, grabbing them just behind the heads and holding them at arm's length for a moment. Then the dancers ran their hands over the snakes from top to bottom to relax the snakes. Looked like mostly rattlesnakes and maybe a couple of bull snakes. Still dancing, the dancers placed the snakes in their mouths. They bit down on the snakes, holding the writhing snakes between their teeth where they had gripped them earlier, just behind their heads.

The hypnotic drumming and chanting went on for what seemed like fifteen or twenty minutes. Everything in the Plaza seemed to pulsate, even the hard rock under their feet. Spellbound, he watched the dancers gyrate, almost as if the dancers were dancing the snakes. He'd read about the Hopi Snake Dance and seen the 1913 B/W video, but none of his research had prepared him for the shocking spectacle of half-naked men dancing around a plaza with rattlesnakes dangling from their mouths.

Both sensational and primitive, the spectacle roused something dark and primordial in him. He couldn't describe it any better than that. Dark and primordial.

Eventually the drums pounded more slowly and the chanting grew quiet, almost a whisper. The dancers made their way out of the Plaza with snakes dangling from their mouths, heading down the various trails that descended from the mesa to the desert landscape below where they would release the snakes into the wild, hoping the snakes would bring rain to the upper world.

When he saw the dancers leaving the Plaza, Jeff struggled with his straw hat while trying to turn off the SpyFocus camera. Same with the iphone camera. By the time he finished he noticed one of the singers pointing to him. Soon others were looking at him and talking. He took that as a sign that he should leave, fast. If you stole its image, you stole the dance and ruined its effect, or so he had been told. Worried, he tried to lose himself in the crowd of onlookers making their way down the one an only actual road that provided access to the mesa. Their cars were parked in multiple lots, both large and small, scattered along the S-shaped road that curved around the mesa and then back again in a gigantic switchback.

A blood red sunset streaked the western sky as he hurried down the dark road to his car, parked in one of the more distant lots because he'd arrived late, after the closer lots had filled. By the time he found his white Ford Taurus most of the cars in the lots had driven by him. Finally, out of breath, he climbed into his Taurus and fired up the gimpy engine, hoping the goddamn thing would start. He knew the engine needed work after his latest oil change. Something about the pistons. He had no idea what the service manager was talking about when he'd picked up his car. The engine turned over several times before finally catching. Then he turned on his lights and pulled out of the parking lot onto the dark road.

As soon as he merged with Highway 265 East he felt safer, more at ease. He checked his rear view mirror and saw the lights of only one vehicle a ways behind him. Highway 265 would take him to I-40, which in turn would take him to I-25 at Albuquerque. From there it was only sixty miles north to Santa Fe. He didn't like to drive long distances at night, but he didn't have much choice tonight. The three hundred miles to Santa Fe would take him just over four hours, by his calculation. His immediate problem was hunger. He hadn't eaten since early this morning.

So he decided to stop at a fast food drive-thru in Ganado, about half way to I-40. He could hold on for another hour or so if necessary.

He noticed the vehicle behind him was closer now, traveling at a speed well above the speed limit. He told himself not to worry, just another car on the road, maybe someone from the dance trying to get home at a decent hour, like him. His headlights barely held back the darkness now, which seemed to deepen the further east he drove. When he checked the rear view mirror again he saw the vehicle behind him was only a few car-lengths away now and gaining. Looked like a Jeep, maybe an old-fashioned two-door Wrangler.

Approaching the rugged Keams Canyon he slowed down to let the Jeep pass. Instead of passing, the Jeep slowed down too, only a car-length behind now. What was that all about?

Suddenly the Jeep leaped forward as if it meant to pass, scrapping his rear bumper.

Jeff fought to control the steering wheel and at the same time stomped on the brake, trying to slow down. Too late. The Jeep bumped the Taurus again, this time clearly on purpose, sending the sputtering Taurus careening to the right.

Jeff screamed as the front right wheel of the Taurus caught the edge of the highway and spun the car out of control. The Taurus rolled once and then hurled over the cliff and plunged down into the dark canyon below.

1

Fernando Lopez had finally decided to cut back his work as a fixer. He'd been loafing around the house for over a week, exhausted by his Peyote Circle case, where he had to chase Joey Alhambra all the way to Red River. This morning he had the house all to himself because his wife Estelle had left early for work at the nonprofit Saint Francis Immigrant Outreach Program, which provided food and clothing and other necessities to the growing immigrant community coming through Santa Fe, a so-called sanctuary city. He was sitting on his patio drinking coffee and admiring Estelle's rose garden when his cell phone rang on the bench beside him. He cursed. He should have left the damn phone inside. But he answered it anyway when he saw the name on the screen: Ruby Montez, one of his oldest friends.

"What's up, Ruby?" he answered.

"Hey, Fernando, I need your help again," Ruby replied. "One of the gals down at my pottery co-op lost her husband the day before yesterday. He was coming back from a dance in Arizona when his car went over a cliff and crashed. Jeff Walker, the photographer. I think you know him."

Fernando did, indeed, know Jeff Walker, who owned a low-rent photography business in a strip mall on Cerrillos Road. He photographed weddings, *quinceañeras*, graduation events, and so forth. He picked up extra money by doing surveillance work for some of the divorce lawyers in town. He'd hired Jeff on two separate cases, both involving people who had disappeared and did not want to be found. Jeff was a decent photographer, if somewhat unreliable.

"Yeah, I know who he is," Fernando said. "I don't think I've never met his wife, though."

"Gail's her name," Ruby said. "She's bereft, as you might imagine."

Fernando sighed. "Okay, but how can I help?"

"Here's the rub," Ruby said. "The Arizona State Police think it was an accident...that Jeff lost control of his car and drove over the cliff. Thing is, they found broken glass close to the skid marks on the highway where Jeff slammed on his brakes. You follow me?"

"So another car might be involved, a car that may have rammed Jeff from behind," Fernando answered. "Is that what you're saying?"

"Exactly," Ruby said. "Can you talk to her?"

Fernando paused. The last thing he wanted to do this morning was get involved with this situation, which would be impossible for him to resolve anyway. Better to let the Arizona State Police handle this. On the other hand, he had a hard time saying no to Ruby, his oldest and dearest friend, which did not set well with Estelle, who disliked Ruby.

"I'll talk to her, but I can't promise anything beyond that," Fernando replied finally.

"Good!" Ruby shot back. "She's with me now at the gallery. You wanna come here, or shall we come over to your house?"

Taken aback, Fernando muttered, "No...I'll come to you...be there shortly."

After Ruby clicked off, Fernando sat for a moment wondering what he could possibly do to 'help' Gail. He for damned sure wasn't about to drive to Arizona to examine glass and skid marks on some highway!

Begrudgingly, Fernando locked up the house and climbed into his Cherokee. He drove down Acequia Madre to the Paseo and around to Canyon Road, then headed up through the shops and art galleries into the artistic center of Santa Fe. He turned into the parking lot between Essentia, a sex shop, and Ruby's gallery, named The Three Cities of Spain after a famous restaurant that had closed years ago. His old office as a private investigator sat back from the road halfway between the two buildings. Now that he called himself a fixer, he worked from home, which suited him just fine. Keep it on the down-low.

He and Ruby were old friends from the culture wars. Her in-your-face personality put off many people but had made her a force in Santa Fe politics for over two decades. A potter by trade, Ruby had risen through the ranks of *La Raza* to become the most progressive member of City Council ever. Back in the 1990s she fought tooth and nail with all the greedy developers who wanted to turn downtown Santa Fe into one big shopping mall. She led rallies, marches, protests, sit-ins, and if you believed the rumors, a fire-bombing or two.

She lost, of course. The developers and the Sotheby's crowd turned Santa Fe into Disneyland Southwest. The tide of gentrification sweeping over Santa Fe during those years hollowed out the city. Gone were most of the people whose families had lived in Santa Fe for generations. Ever higher home values and property taxes priced out all who couldn't afford million dollar homes. After two tumultuous terms on City Council lecturing, berating, cajoling, and threatening the other members, Ruby said 'fuck it' and retired to the pottery co-op she owned and ran with a number of other potters, all of them women.

Ruby inherited her Canyon Road studio from her ex-husband, Jimmy Mackey. Jimmy was a painter with a modest reputation in Santa Fe and northern New Mexico who was murdered in a raunchy sex scandal involving a host of Canyon Road artists as well as the then mayor of Santa Fe and his estranged wife. Fortunately for Fernando, the studio came with a detached garage that needed an occupant at about the same time he resigned as chief detective on the Santa Fe Police Department and decided to set up office as a private investigator.

The arrangement worked well for both of them. Especially for Fernando, since Ruby had never charged him rent, only utilities. He had no idea what Ruby got out of the arrangement. Security? Companionship? She liked having him next door, someone to listen to her diatribes, for sure. Must be something like that because Ruby kept trying to convince him to reopen the office and resume his work as a private investigator. He'd thought about coming back for a while, but realized finally he preferred to keep a low profile and be more selective in taking on new cases as a fixer, cleaning up other people's messes. God knows there were enough people with messes to keep him in business as long as he wanted to work.

Fernando parked next to Ruby's blue Honda Accord. He noticed the red Nissan Sentra parked on the other side of the Honda and figured it must belong to Gail Walker. He walked up to the porch and opened the door. When he stepped inside, he entered a proverbial riot of color, with bright abstract canvases hanging on the walls and just as bright ceramics arranged on shelves toward the rear of the gallery. He could hear muffled voices coming from the small room off to the side that Ruby called her lunchroom, so he walked on back.

Gail Walker sat next to the counter, with a box of tissues in front of her. A heavy-set buxom blond with long hair wound in a lose bun on top of her head, she glanced up at him and burst into tears.

"Sorry to disappoint you," Fernando said. He often had that effect on people. Why, he had no idea.

"Hi Fernando," Ruby announced loudly, ending the awkward moment. "This is Gail. Thanks for coming."

Gail dabbed at her eyes with a handful of tissues. She wore shorts and a skimpy halter top, even though summer had long since peaked. "Sorry...I'm just a holy mess today."

"Not a problem," Fernando said, taking the third seat at the end of the counter near the mini fridge and the microwave. "Why don't you tell me what you know about your husband's accident?"

"That's the thing," Gail sniffed. "I'm not sure it was an accident. I told him not to go...driving three hundred miles...the money's not worth it."

"Where exactly in Arizona did he go?" Fernando asked. "Ruby said a dance of some sort?"

Gail nodded, getting her composure back. "He went all the way to the Hopi Reservation to film the Snake Dance."

Surprised, Fernando shook his head. "The Hopi Snake Dance is closed to outsiders. Has been for years. There's no way he could have filmed the dance—at least not legally."

"Not only that—there's a curse on any outsiders who come to Hopi intending to steal the Snake Dance," Ruby added. "I know that from my experience with Jimmy. He snuck into the dance one year with a bunch of hippies and later tried to paint it. After that he had nothing but bad luck. He always blamed the curse of the Snake Dance for bringing him the bad luck."

Gail shrugged. "All I know's what Jeff told me. He said someone at the Santa Fe Film Collective was offering him a lot of money, but he didn't say who. He hadn't been doing very well lately. Things are expensive in Santa Fe. Money's tight. People don't like to spend a lot of money on photo shoots anymore. They can just take their own pictures with their cell phones."

"Ain't that the truth," Ruby interjected. "People are always showing me family photos on their damn cell phones. I'm tired of looking at them."

Fernando paused, trying to think of a way to ask his next question without upsetting Gail. Not easy. He cleared his throat. "Have the authorities in Arizona made arrangements for your husband's remains to be sent back to Santa Fe?"

Huge tears rolled down Gail's cheeks.

Ruby answered for Gail. "The body arrived yesterday. I'm helping with the mortuary and the visitation and all that."

Fernando nodded. "What about his effects? His belongings?"

This time Gail answered. "Yes, they arrived in a box yesterday. I haven't opened it yet."

"Would you mind if I came over and took a look?" Fernando asked. "The contents might tell us more about what happened, I don't know."

"You're welcome to come over and open the box," Gail said. "I just haven't had the courage."

Gail wrote her address on a napkin and passed it to Fernando. "Come over this afternoon, if you want. I need to stop at Kaune's, but I'll be home the rest of the afternoon."

In turn, Fernando handed her one of his business cards. "I'm no longer a private investigator, but my phone number is the same."

With that, Gail thanked Ruby and got up to leave. Ruby gave her a big hug and walked her to the front door of the gallery.

When she returned to the lunch room, Ruby shook her head angrily. "She's in a bad way—emotionally and financially. Jeff was a fucking loser. To make matters worse, he had a gambling problem...spent way too much time at the casinos. He didn't leave her with a life insurance policy or anything else. She has no savings, nada. And now she has to find a way to bury the sonofabitch. Just to have him cremated will cost nearly ten thousand dollars. I'm gonna have to do a fund raiser for her at the pottery co-op. Try to raise some money fast."

"Estelle and I will make a contribution," Fernando said.

"Thanks," Ruby said. "So what do you think? Can you help?"

"Let's take a look at what's in that box," Fernando said, avoiding the question.

2

On the way home Fernando thought of a way he might help Gail. He had an old friend, Arturo Naranjo, who'd retired a few years earlier than he did from the Santa Fe Police Department. Originally from Arizona, Arturo moved back to a small Arizona town called Jeddito when he retired. Jeddito happened to be only a few miles east of Keams Canyon, as he recalled. Maybe Arturo could provide more information about what happened on that mountain road the night Jeff Walker ran off the road and fell into the canyon.

He went into his study and found his ancient address book, held together by a rubber band. The binding had broken years ago, but he'd never taken the time to replace it. Probably because half the people in the address book were dead, the others were well on their way. He found Arturo's address and phone number on the very last page, in the Z section. Why Z, he had no idea.

Arturo answered on the first ring, as punctual as Fernando remembered him. "Who's calling, please?"

"Arturo, it's Fernando Lopez from Santa Fe...you might remember me from our time together at the Washington Avenue Station."

"Of course! Fernando, how the hell are you?" Arturo replied.

"I'm okay," Fernando said. "I retired a few years ago and since then have been doing some private work."

"Good for you. Got to keep busy."

"I'm calling to ask if you know anything about this photographer from Santa Fe who drove off the cliff driving through Keams Canyon," Fernando said. "Did you hear about this?"

"Yeah...I read something about it in the newspaper, why?"

"His wife is distraught, she doesn't think it was an accident," Fernando replied. "She thinks he was forced off the road."

"I see."

"So I wondered if you would be willing to take a look," Fernando continued. "Apparently there are skid marks and glass where the photographer—Jeff Walker—went over the cliff."

"Sure, I can take a look, I know exactly where it happened," Arturo said. "I could even take a look at the car. I think it's still in the canyon in a hard to reach place. There's a county road into the canyon that would get me close—I could walk the rest of the way. No problem."

"I'd really appreciate it," Fernando said. "And Jeff's wife would be grateful."

"Not a problem. I'll take a look and call you back later today," Arturo said.

"Thanks, I owe you one," Fernando said and clicked off.

He felt better knowing that Arturo would take a look at the evidence. He trusted Arturo, who'd been one of his most reliable colleagues during the years he'd worked at the Santa Fe Police Department.

Fernando ate a light lunch and then took a look at the napkin Gail had given him. He had no idea where her house was located. Maez Road, off Cerrillos. He'd never heard of the neighborhood, if you could call it a neighborhood. He waited until nearly one o'clock before leaving. He took the Paseo around to Cerrillos Road and turned left. He passed by the aging strip mall where Jeff Walker had his studio. Maez Road turned out to be three long blocks down Cerrillos, a pseudo-residential area of small houses and run-down properties.

He followed Gail's directions down a side street to a small cinderblock house painted light blue with a carport instead of a garage. A weed-infested lawn circled the house on three sides, while a high cinderblock wall blocked the rear of the property, which bordered an alley. Fernando parked behind Gail's red Sentra and walked up to the house.

Gail opened the front door as soon as he rang the bell, as if she were waiting for him inside. He noticed she'd exchanged her shorts and halter top for a yellow cotton dress.

"Come in," she said. "I'm sorry I'm such a mess."

"No, it's understandable," Fernando replied. "You just lost your husband."

She led him into a small front room with a sofa and chairs arranged around a brick fireplace. Family photos hung on all the walls. Fernando assumed they were from Jeff's studio.

Gail pointed to the dining room table, where an unopened box and a pair of scissors sat waiting. Looked like she had gone to open the box and then changed her mind at the last minute.

Gail stood back staring at the box. "I don't know why, but I'm afraid to open the package. Will you open it for me?"

"Sure, no problem," Fernando said. He walked to the table and looked at the box, a standard 24x18x12 cardboard box with a label on the front. He ignored the scissors and instead took out his pocket knife and sliced through the packing tape.

When he opened the box, he spotted a wallet, sunglasses, and an iphone on top of a pile of clothes and a smashed straw hat. He took these items out of the box and laid them carefully on the table. Underneath the clothing he found a flashlight, papers from the glove compartment, and a few tools, including a screwdriver, several wrenches, and a pair of pliers.

Gail watched from across the room, refusing to come any closer. As if the contents of the box were haunted.

"Does all this look familiar?" Fernando asked.

"I guess," she said. "The clothing and the straw hat, anyway."

When Fernando picked up the straw hat, a pocket notebook fell out from under it. "Would you mind if I take a look at this?" Fernando asked, holding up the notebook for her to see.

"Help yourself, I don't want it."

Fernando put the notebook in his back pocket and pried open the smashed straw hat. What he found inside surprised him. Someone, Jeff obviously, had cut a hole in the hat and duck-taped a small video camera to the inside of the front brim, its lens facing out. Ingenious, really. Jeff could videotape the snake dance without being noticed. All he would have to do would be to turn facing whatever he wanted to record.

Fernando showed Gail the hidden camera. "He hid the camera in his hat so he could photograph surreptitiously."

"Oh, I don't like that word, surreptitiously. Sounds illegal," Gail said.

"Can I borrow the camera for a while?"

Gail nodded.

Fernando placed the hat on the table and held up the cell phone.

"Do you know the passcode to Jeff's cell phone?"

"Yeah, it's his birthday: eleven, twenty-one, nineteen sixty-five," Gail replied.

"I'll need to look at the cell phone, but I will return it," Fernando said. "I promise."

Again Gail nodded. "Take what you want. I don't want any of it."

"Okay...you're right about the illegality issue," Fernando said. "The snake dance is closed to outsiders, so the hidden videotaping would be considered illegal. Someone may have seen Jeff filming, or suspected him of filming, and then pursued him after the dance. That stretch of highway coming into Keams Canyon is treacherous. If a car came up fast behind Jeff and side-swiped his car, or rammed it on purpose, that could have sent him over the edge of the cliff."

"So it might not be an accident," Gail said.

"Well, I don't know at this point, I'm just saying it could have been retribution for videotaping the dance," Fernando said. "Murder, in other words."

Before leaving, Fernando gave her another of his business cards. "Call me if you can think of anything else. I'll be in touch."

With that, he walked out of the house and climbed into his Cherokee. He drove straight home, wanting to take a look at the camera and iphone immediately to get a sense of what he was dealing with.

As soon as he walked into his kitchen, he made himself another cup of coffee and carried it into his study. He took the SpyFocus camera and Jeff's iphone out of his pockets and deposited them next to his laptop. He had no idea how a SpyFocus camera worked, so he googled the camera and read everything he could find. He discovered the camera worked by connecting to a Wi-Fi network using an app, which he didn't have. Even if he downloaded the app, he wouldn't have Jeff's password.

Fernando put aside the camera, planning to come back later if he could get Jeff's password from Gail. At the moment he wanted to check out Jeff's iphone. He typed in the passcode Gail had shared with him and booted up the phone. First he wanted to take a look at Jeff's email to learn more about who was paying him to film the mysterious Hopi Snake Dance. Unfortunately, access to the email account required a password, which he didn't have. That would have to wait.

Next, he clicked the photo icon on the iphone' screen. A list of Jeff's photos and videos appeared. Sure enough, the first filename read: "Snake Dance." Before he had a chance to click the play button, his cell phone rang.

"Mister Lopez, I'm so sorry," Gail Walker said, speaking fast, "but could you bring back Jeff's iphone and camera? Something's come up and I need them right away. I'm so sorry to call you like this. I just...I just don't know what to do. Could you please bring them back?"

Taken aback, Fernando asked. "Why? What's wrong?"

"Please! I can't say any more. Please bring them back," she said and clicked off.

Fernando sat at his desk, stunned. Obviously Gail must be under pressure by someone who wanted those videos badly.

Before leaving for Gail's house, he sent the video to his email account. He would get back to the video as soon as he could. As soon as he found out why Gail had changed her mind.

3

As he turned from Cerrilllos Road onto Maez, Fernando wondered if he should have brought his Smith & Wesson. He hadn't strapped on the big gun for over a week now. He'd decided against it, not wanting to overreact. When Gail's house came into view, he saw her car parked in the same place as before. She hadn't gone anywhere. The trouble, whatever had made her change her mind about giving him the iphone and camera, had come knocking on her door.

Gail once again opened the door before he could ring the bell. "Come in—quick," she said, looking around outside.

"Whoa, what's the hurry," Fernando said as she pulled him inside.

"They might be watching," she said, closing and locking the door behind Fernando. "I'm a nervous wreck. They threatened me if I don't give them what they want, the video. But I don't know where it is...on the iphone or the camera. I don't know anything about it. What'll I do?"

"Here, I'll show you," Fernando said, taking Jeff's iphone out of his pocket and handing it to her. "Jeff shot a video of the dance using his cell phone camera. Just tap on the Photos icon and you'll see it. There may be another copy on the small camera he'd placed inside his hat—I don't know for sure because I don't have the app or the password to download the film."

Gail nodded, looking at the cell phone she held in her hand.

"Here, I'll put the camera on your dining room table with the other stuff," Fernando said. That's when he noticed the disarray in the dining room. Someone had taken the contents out of the shipping box and tossed them randomly on the table, even the floor. No wonder Gail was worried.

"So who did this? Who are these guys?" Fernando asked.

"They want the video," Gail said. "They paid Jeff ten thousand dollars to go to Arizona and videotape the dance."

"Yeah, but who are they? Do you have their names?"

Gail shook her head. "They're from the Santa Fe Film Collective. That's all I know. They didn't tell me their names."

"Well, then, what did they look like?" Fernando replied, losing patience with her. "Give me something that might help identify them."

"Two middle-aged men, maybe in their fifties," she said. "The one who did the talking was tall and handsome with dark hair and a goatee. He wore slacks and s dress shirt. The other guy was shorter and heavier. He wore jeans and a Western shirt with snaps, you know, not buttons."

"Okay—did they already pay your husband the ten thousand dollars?" Fernando asked.

"Yes, I checked the bank. The money was deposited a few days ago."

Fernando nodded. "Then I would just give them the two cameras and be rid of them. If you want to keep Jeff's iphone, you can send them the video by email. It's simple."

Gail considered. After a long pause, she said, "I wonder. If they wanted a video of the dance bad enough to give Jeff ten thousand dollars in advance, how much would they pay now, to actually get their hands on the video?"

Fernando raised his hands. "My advice would be to give them the video and be done with it. First of all, you can't do anything else with the tape because secretly videotaping a private Hopi Snake Dance is illegal. Second, these guys could be dangerous. Why take a chance?"

Gail did not respond. Ignoring Fernando, she carried Jeff's iphone into the front room and sat on her sofa to view the video. She clicked on the fast forward button and watched in silence. Then she clicked on the play button when she came to the part of the video where the Snake Dancers came forward and grabbed the snakes. "Oh my God!" she said, turning to Fernando. "Have you watched this?"

"I have," Fernando replied, even though he'd only seen the first image.

"I can't believe they actually do this," she said, returning to the video.

Fernando realized he had Jeff Walker's notebook in his pocket. He'd forgotten to look at it earlier. He took out the notebook and thumbed through it, seeing nothing to do with the Hopi Snake Dance. Then he placed it on the dining room table with the other stuff, wanting to be rid of it.

Gail continued to ignore him while she watched the video, so Fernando took the opportunity to leave. He walked out of the house shaking his head, not knowing what else he could do for her.

He climbed into his Cherokee and drove back to Cerrillos Road, glad to be away from Gail Walker, who seemed to have forgotten about her dead husband. Whatever. He wanted to forget about the lot of them.

Fernando ignored the commercial claptrap on Cerrillos Road and then took the Paseo around to Acequia Madre. Once back at his house he decided to resume his newfound life of leisure, so he made himself another cup of coffee and took it out to the patio.

His cell phone rang just as he sat down on the bench. He clicked accept when he saw Arturo's name.

"Fernando...it's Arturo," his old friend said. "I just got back from Keams Canyon. Walker's car is still there, smashed almost beyond recognition. I did notice some gray paint on the left bumper and some glass above where he went off the highway, so it is possible that another car caused the accident, deliberately. There's no way to tell for sure, but I wouldn't be surprised if one of the Hopi had seen him filming and came after him."

"Thanks, Arturo, that's about what I expected," Fernando said. "Sounds like they may have gone after him. We'll probably never know for sure."

After clicking off, he put the cell phone away and finished his coffee. Sitting on the patio, his mind kept returning to the Hopi Snake Dance and the purloined video—in spite of himself. He'd read several ethnographic descriptions of the Snake Dance and seen the black and white photos the ethnographers had shot. And he'd read perhaps the most famous description of the dance by the English novelist D. H. Lawrence collected in *Mornings in Mexico*, a collection of Lawrence's writings from the mid-1920s. Part of that time Lawrence lived outside of Taos at a ranch Mabel Dodge Luhan had given him and his wife Frieda, supposedly in exchange for one of his manuscripts. As crazy as that sounded.

Lawrence's mystical interpretation of the Snake Dance made for great reading for those so inclined. Fernando wasn't so inclined, but he'd always admired Lawrence's attempt to capture a Native American perspective on life and the cosmos, where everything is alive and moving.

A few minutes later Fernando went back in the house. Thinking about Lawrence's portrait of the Snake Dance, he decided to reread Lawrence's description. He hadn't seen the book in years, so he didn't exactly know where to find the book. He looked first in the bedroom, among the piles of books Estelle liked to read in bed. Lots of books about New Mexico and by New Mexican writers. Estelle's favorite was John Nichols. She'd read *The Milagro Beanfield War* several times. But he didn't find the Lawrence book there or in the big bookshelf in their living room. Desperate, he went back into his study and rummaged through his closet. He finally found the book, with a torn cover and dog-eared pages, stuffed in a brown paper bag filled with stuff to be thrown away on the floor in one corner of the closet.

He sat down in his desk chair and began reading the torn and tattered book. Lawrence had attended the Hopi Snake Dance in 1924 with about 3,000 other visitors, according to Lawrence's account. Back then the dance was public and apparently very popular, more as a sensational spectacle than a religious ritual. When the ceremony begins, Lawrence describes the heavy rhythmic chanting in his usual mystical mumbo-jumbo:

"It is a strange low sound, such as we never hear, and it reveals how deep, how deep the men are in the mystery they are practicing, how sunk deep below our world, to the world of snakes, and dark ways in the earth, where are the roots of corn, and where the little rivers of unchannelled [*sic*], uncreated life-passion run like dark, trickling lightning, to the roots of the corn and to the feet and loins of the men, from the earth's innermost dark sun. They are calling in the deep, almost silent snake-language, to the snakes and the rays of dark emission from the earth's inward 'Sun.'"

"Dark emission from the earth's inward 'Sun'"? What the hell was that? Not Fernando's cup of tea.

Lawrence's description was so vague that Fernando decided to see for himself. He would watch the purloined video one time and then forget about the damn thing. So he took out his cell phone and booted up the video Jeff had secretly recorded. He clicked the play button and sat back in his chair.

At first the video was dark and wobbly, as if Jeff was moving around trying to find a better vantage point, but quickly the focus kicked in and the movement stabilized. What he saw interested him more than he thought it would: a group of twelve dancers coming out of a kiva. They wore their hair long with feathers, with lots of black and white paint on their naked torsos and leather breeches. They danced around a Plaza to the pounding drumming and chanting from a group of singers near the kiva. Fernando was surprised by the clarity of the iphone video, even as the evening light began to dim and shadows began to appear in the Plaza area behind the dancers. The shadows gave great depth and a sense of noir to the proceedings, which seemed somehow illicit. This lasted for several minutes.

Then the dramatic moment came. The dancers approached the underground crypt near the kiva where the snakes were kept. One by one the dancers reached in and grabbed a snake. They held the snakes out away from their bodies and then plunged them into their mouths, griping the writhing serpents between their teeth. Like this they continued dancing, snakes dangling from their mouths. Stunned, Fernando could not take his eyes off the half-naked men dancing around the Plaza with snakes writhing in their mouths. There was something raw or elemental about the spectacle that made it so powerful, so hard to stop watching. He didn't want to use the term primitive. That would be insulting to the Hopi.

He hit the stop button. He'd seen enough. Now he understood why the video would be a gold mind to people in the film industry. Images this sensational would be easy to monetize. Leave it to Hollywood.

4

Next morning Fernando downloaded the Snake Dance video onto his laptop and played it for Estelle. He was trying to explain his latest case, if you could call it a case, and thought the video would help. To understand, you had to actually see a man dancing while dangling a snake between his teeth. Fernando watched her closely for her reaction as she viewed the video.

"Yes, this is amazing," Estelle said, shaking her head. She looked incredibly youthful this morning, with her rich olive skin contrasting beautifully with her short silver hair. In truth, she'd aged much better than he had. Still slim and fit, she walked every day during her lunch hour and sometimes again in the evening after dinner. She could be a model of how to age well. Fernando, not so much. Too much stress and physical abuse over the years, thanks to thirty years in law enforcement and another five as a private investigator and then a fixer. Nothing much he could do about that. It came with the territory.

Estelle turned back to Fernando. "But where did you get this? The Hopi Snake Dance is closed to visitors. It's illegal to record it, I think."

"Did you see the *Independent* story about Jeff Walker? The Santa Fe photographer who ran off the highway coming back from Arizona?"

Estelle nodded. "I skimmed it."

"Well, he was coming back from secretly recording the Hopi Snake Dance on First Mesa. It was either an accident or someone ran him off the highway. I'm not sure we'll ever know which."

"So how come you have it on your computer?"

"Arizona State Police sent Jeff's belongings back to his wife Gail, who let me borrow the iphone Jeff used to record the dance," Fernando said. "I took the liberty of sending the video to myself."

"Wait. How did you get involved in this? You don't know the Walkers."

"Gail's one of the potters who work at Ruby's co-op. Ruby asked me to help her," Fernando said.

"Hah! Your girlfriend again. I might have known she was involved," Estelle said. She grabbed her lunch and headed for the kitchen door on her way to work. She stopped at the door and turned to face Fernando. "Just remember this. You're supposed to be retired. You told me after the last case that you wouldn't take any more. And yet, here you are."

With that, Estelle turned away and walked out the door. Moments later Fernando heard her Camry start and then drive off on Acequia Madre.

"That went well," he said out loud, unable to refrain from his usual sarcasm when he and Estelle talked about retirement. The irony was that she worked every day at her volunteer nonprofit, whereas he only worked intermittently. The difference, according to Estelle, was that what she did was service, not work. He remained dubious about the distinction.

After Estelle left, Fernando went for a long, leisurely walk on Acequia Madre. When he returned he did the unthinkable: took a nap. A light lunch followed the nap, after which he went into his study to work on the genealogy project he'd been working on for the past several months. When finished, he wanted to give copies to both of his daughters, Adela and Flavia.

He opened his laptop, but before he could boot it up his cell phone rang on the desk. He saw the name on the screen and immediately began to worry. Every time Manny Alvarez called, it meant big trouble. Manny had replaced him as lead detective on the Santa Fe Police Department and called him routinely about police activity. Sometimes Manny asked for his advice, sometimes not.

"Fernando, do you know a Gail Walker?" Manny asked.

Fernando's spirits sank, expecting the worst. "Why?"

"Because we found your card next to her phone," Manny replied.

"Where's Gail?"

Manny sighed. "She's in her living room with an electric cord wrapped around her neck. Dead."

Fernando did not respond.

"So how do you know this woman? Why did she have your card beside her phone?"

"It's a long story," Fernando said. "Are you at her house now?"

"Yes, waiting for Forensics."

"I'm on my way," Fernando said and then clicked off. He quickly locked up the house and climbed into his Cherokee, racing around the Paseo to Cerrillos Road. When he turned right on Maez, he saw Manny's cruiser parked behind Gail's red Sentra. The Forensics van still hadn't arrived.

Fernando parked on the street to give Forensics more room to park in the narrow drive and walked up to the small house. The door hung ajar, as if it had been forcibly opened. As soon as he stepped inside he saw the damage. The front sitting room and dining room had been ransacked, cabinets and drawers opened, their contents thrown out on the bare wooden floor. Sofa cushions, chairs, everything in the rooms had been displaced or overturned. Looked like a tornado had ripped through the entire house leaving nothing but carnage.

Then he spotted Gail's body behind the sofa, next to a smashed lamp. The electric cord had been pulled out of the lamp and wrapped around Gail's neck and tightened. She lay on her back, her face purple and bloated and her empty eyes looking up at the ceiling. Barefoot, she wore the same yellow cotton dress he'd seen her wearing yesterday. Not a pretty sight.

Fernando turned away, having seen enough. He saw Manny in the kitchen, going through the broken dishes and piles of pots and pans thrown haphazardly on the counters and the floor.

Manny walked out of the kitchen and threw up his arms. "What the hell happened here? What were they looking for?"

"Like I said, it's a long story. Here, sit down," he said, pointing to a couple of chairs in the living room, about the only two pieces of furniture untouched by the vandals.

Manny took a seat beside Fernando. A clean-cut, forty-something bachelor with a bird-like face and impeccably trimmed hair and moustache, Manny had grown into his job as lead detective. Formerly known as a wise-ass, he was now just fussy and sometimes quarrelsome.

Fernando pointed to Gail's body on the floor. "I take it you know about the death of Gail's husband, Jeff Walker. He's the photographer who died when his car ran off the road and over a cliff in Arizona near Keams Canyon. The Arizona State Police aren't sure if it was an accident or if he was run off the road intentionally by another vehicle. Anyway, it turns out that Jeff was returning to Santa Fe from the Hopi Reservation. He'd been paid ten thousand dollars to secretly videotape the Hopi Snake Dance on First Mesa."

"Wait a minute, the Hopi Snake Dance is closed to the public," Manny interrupted.

"I know, that's why Jeff had to tape it surreptitiously, using a hidden camera and his iphone," Fernando replied. "Both his camera and iphone were returned to Gail the day before yesterday. I helped her unpack the box."

"So have you seen the video, then?" Manny asked.

Fernando raised his hand to slow Manny down. "Yes, I emailed myself a copy. I have it on my iphone if you want to take a look."

"I do, but finish the story," Manny said. "Are you saying this video was why Gail was murdered and the house ransacked?"

"Exactly. People connected to the Santa Fe Film Collective paid Jeff to record the video and wanted what they'd paid for, but Gail was planning to ask them for more money. That's the last I heard from her."

Manny stood up and looked around. "Doesn't look like they found what they were looking for."

"No, it doesn't," Fernando replied.

Manny walked through the entire house looking at the overturned furniture and empty cabinets. Then he returned to the kitchen, where everything had been removed from the overhead cabinets and tossed on the floor. Finally he gave up and came back to the chairs. "So who are these people from the Santa Fe Film Collective? Did Gail have any names?"

Fernando shook his head. "No, just a description of the two."

Manny passed his notebook to Fernando. "Write down the descriptions."

Fernando did as he was told and passed the notebook back.

"Now, let me see the video," Manny said, sitting down in his chair.

Fernando took out his cell phone and booted up the video. He passed his cell phone to Manny and sat down in the other chair.

Manny watched the video, his face grim. When the Hopis began dancing with snakes dangling from their mouths, he said, "Aww, Christ! I can't watch this. It's disgusting!"

"It's part of their religion," Fernando replied.

"I know...I know," Manny said, stopping the video and handing the cell phone back to Fernando.

Just then they heard a siren approaching on the street outside. The Forensics van was arriving.

Manny got up to meet the van. He turned to Fernando. "Do the people who did this know you have a copy of the video?"

"Not that I'm aware of," Fernando said.

"Good," Manny replied. "You might want to keep that on the down-low."

5

On the way back home Fernando began to worry. He hadn't considered the possibility that whoever killed Gail might suspect he had a copy of the video. But why not? His business card was out in plain sight beside Gail's desk phone. If Manny found it there, why not the killer or killers?

Rattled, Fernando turned onto Acequia Madre Street and looked to make sure there were no strange vehicles parked in his driveway. There weren't, so he pulled up to his garage and quickly went into the house.

He wanted to keep his mind busy, so he walked into his study and booted up his laptop to continue working on his genealogy project. His father's side of the family had been easy. He could trace the Lopez family history in New Mexico back to 1630, the year Salvador de Lopez, originally of Valladolid, Spain, came to Santa Fe. A soldier and a blacksmith by trade, Salvador accompanied a mission supply train up the El Camino Real trail from Mexico City to Santa Fe, which had been founded in 1610.

His mother's side of the family history—the McCarthy side—had been more difficult to trace. Originally from Boston, his mother's parents had moved to Albuquerque after World War II. Annie Lee McCarthy, their only child, had married Fernando's father, Amerigo Lopez, in 1962 when they were both students at the University of New Mexico. Fernando was born the following year. He was searching for more information on the McCarthy family in Boston when his cell phone rang on the desk, interrupting his concentration.

Fernando froze when he saw the local but unknown number.

The phone rang twice, three times before he clicked on.

"We want the video," a deep voice intoned on the other end. "We know you have it. We know where you live on Acequia Madre. You can bring the video to us...or we'll come get it."

Fernando steadied his nerves. The man's attitude pissed him off. He didn't respond to that tone of voice. "No, don't come over here. Who are you and where are you located?"

"Name's Max Russo," the man replied. "I'm the owner of Santa Fe Film Collective. You can find me at the Santa Fe Armory for the Arts on Old Pecos Trail. We're the last office near the back door. Bring the video."

The line went dead.

Fernando sat in his chair brooding. He did, in fact, have a copy of the video, but not the original video on Jeff Walker's cell phone or the one on his SpyFocus camera, both of which had seemingly disappeared. Should he share his copy of the video with Russo? Or at least let Russo watch it? That was the question.

Feeling agitated, unable to concentrate on anything else, he headed for the door. After locking the house, he climbed into his Cherokee and drove to the Paseo and around to Old Santa Fe Trail. Then he bore right on Old Pecos Trail and soon came to the Santa Fe Armory of the Arts, one of several sprawling buildings that had been built in the 1930s to train National Guard units.

Fernando pulled into the parking lot of the building that housed the current Santa Fe Armory for the Arts. A large open structure that looked like a store-front, the adobe building displayed a new coat of the typical Santa Fe brown stucco. Inside the spacious lobby, he saw a few people talking quietly over by the office of a city theater troupe. He continued on down a long hallway toward the back of the building, where he came to a sign that read "Santa Fe Film Collective."

He opened the heavy wooden door and stepped into the small office, its walls decorated with colorful posters of movies filmed in New Mexico. He recognized posters for *Silverado, Young Guns, 3:10 to Yuma, Oppenheimer,* and *Rez Ball.* A muscular, pretty-boy who looked like a wannabe cowboy sat at a desk wearing a black western shirt with pearl buttons. With shaggy hair and a bushy moustache, he glanced over the copy of the *Independent* he was reading and asked, "Can I help you?"

Fernando frowned, taking an instant dislike to the cowboy. "Are you Max Russo?"

The cowboy shook his head. "Like I said, can I help you?"

"I'm here about the video," Fernando said. "I got a call from somebody here...."

Cowboy pointed to what looked like the inner office. "He's in there."

Fernando walked into a back office surrounded by bookshelves from floor to ceiling on all four walls. The shelves were stacked with reels of film, videocassettes, books, and what looked like loosely-bound scripts.

In the center of the room a man sat at one end of a long conference table with a cell phone and a laptop on the table. Professionally dressed, he wore slacks, a button down shirt, and a bolo tie. The bolo tie had a silver slide inlaid with a turquoise stone as large as a golf ball. Expensive.

"Max Russo?" Fernando asked, looking at the man's weathered face. He looked to be at least sixty years old, maybe more.

The man nodded. "Did you bring the video?"

"I don't have it," Fernando said. "I helped Gail Walker unpack the box of her husband's belongings. We found a SpyFocus camera and a cell phone. I left both on the dining room table. You should have found them when you murdered her."

Russo stared at Fernando, not speaking. "No, they were gone," he said finally, ignoring the murder allegation.

"You do know that the Hopi Snake Dance is closed to the public—all photographing is illegal," Fernando continued.

"So I'm told," Russo said, still staring at Fernando.

"Why do you want it?" Fernando asked. "What can you do with it?"

The question made Russo smile. "Right now we have one director—René Durand—who's willing to pay two hundred grand for a two-minute clip of the Hopi Snake Dance. He's from France or Belgium, one of those French-speaking countries. You have no idea how many directors would pay dearly for a small clip of the Snake Dance to incorporate in their movies. Documentaries, commercials, you name it. The possibilities are endless for something like this. There's nothing else like it anywhere, you understand? It's one of a kind."

"So that's why you murdered Gail Walker," Fernando said. "Did you murder Jeff too?"

Russo sighed, ignoring Fernando's question. "I want you to bring me the video. We'll pay you a finder's fee, so to speak."

"I told you, I don't have the video," Fernando said.

"You will," Russo said and then looked around on his desk. When he found what he was looking for, he passed a piece of paper to Fernando: a UPS receipt for a package Gail sent to Fernando's address on Acequia Madre Street. Mailed the day she was murdered.

This was news to Fernando. Not good news. He crumpled the receipt and threw it on the table.

"Bring it to me when it arrives...or I will come and get it."

Fernando did not like to be threatened. He balled his fists. He moved closer to the conference table and looked down at Russo. Then he grabbed Russo's bolo tie and pulled it to the side, tight around his neck.

"Stay away from my house," Fernando hissed. "If you come near it, I'll kill you." With that he released the bolo tie and shoved Russo back in his chair.

By this time the wannabe cowboy in front had heard the ruckus and appeared in the doorway. He glared at Fernando. "Do you want me to take care of this guy?" he asked Russo.

Russo brought his hand up to his mouth and coughed. "That won't be necessary, Wes. He's leaving now."

Fernando walked to the door, partially blocked by cowboy Wes. He pushed cowboy back out of the way with his forearm and walked out of the office. For just a moment he thought cowboy would take a swipe at him, which would have given Fernando the great pleasure of planting a fist in pretty-boy's face.

He walked down the hallway and out the front door, stopping a moment to bask in the sun. He took a long, slow breath. Like it or not, he found himself deeply involved in this messy affair.

All he could think about at the moment was what, if anything, to tell Estelle. Should he warn her that these people might show up at their home? Estelle had already given him warning that if he asked her to go stay with one of their daughters one more time, she would leave him for good. He hadn't taken her seriously, but he didn't want to press his luck.

One thing he knew for certain. Estelle was sick and tired of the trouble that seemed to follow him everywhere like a damn shadow!

6

Fernando and Estelle went outside to sit on the patio after dinner. They watched the fireflies begin to flicker under the big cottonwood trees and listened to the locusts starting up their evening hum. All through dinner Fernando had debated whether to tell Estelle more about the Snake Dance murder investigation and the possible threat from Max Russo and his pretty-boy companion, Wes. He couldn't decide what to do, so he'd said nothing.

Both he and Estelle enjoyed sitting on the patio after dinner. They purchased their 1920s adobe on Acequia Madre Street early in their marriage. They'd preserved the small adobe pretty much as it was when they bought it, except for minor modernizations. He took great pride in preserving this small piece of history on a street blighted by gentrification. Up and down Acequia Madre wealthy newcomers had bought and remodeled the houses into million-dollar mansions. The over-class, he called them, rich people who had turned Santa Fe into Disneyland Southwest. As a result long-time Santa Feans could no longer afford to live in Santa Fe. The median price of a house in Santa Fe County was approaching one million dollars. He didn't consider himself a class warrior, but clearly something had to be done. The economic disparities here, as everywhere else, had become obscene.

While they chatted, a brown panel truck turned into their driveway. Fernando recognized a UPS truck. The truck parked beside his Cherokee and the driver jumped out with a small package in his hand. He headed for the kitchen door and then saw Fernando and Estelle sitting on the patio in the semi-darkness. "Oh...didn't see you there," the driver said, a young man wearing the brown UPS uniform. He handed the package to Fernando.

"Thanks," Fernando said, as the young man turned and walked back to the panel truck.

Fernando and Estelle watched the truck drive off, heading down Acequia Madre to the Paseo. "What's that?" Estelle asked after the truck left.

Fernando felt like the proverbial deer caught in headlights. "I think it's the cell phone and camera Jeff Walker used to film the Hopi Snake Dance before his death. His wife, Gail, sent them to me to keep them out of the hands of the people who paid Jeff to film the dance."

Estelle gave him the Evil Eye. "Well send them back, I don't want them here if these guys are looking for it."

Fernando shook his head. "I wish I could, but I can't."

Estelle stared at him. "Why can't you?"

Fernando sighed. "Because she's dead."

"Dead? What do you mean?"

"They murdered her," Fernando said, regretting his honesty the moment he spoke because he knew what Estelle's reaction would be.

Estelle shot up from the bench. "You brought what Jeff Walker's wife's murderers were looking for here—to our home? What's wrong with you?" she yelled and rushed into the house.

Fernando waited a few minutes, giving Estelle time to calm down. Then he took the package into the kitchen and opened it on the kitchen table. No surprises. Both the SpyFocus camera and Jeff Walker's cell phone were inside. No note of any kind had been included. He couldn't make up his mind what to do with the package. Should he keep it, or should he take it to Manny tomorrow morning and tell him everything that had happened?

For safekeeping, he put the package on the top shelf of the kitchen pantry, behind a large bag of flour, and then went down the hallway to their bedroom. He undressed as quietly as possible and then scooted in to bed next to Estelle. She rolled away, turning her back to him.

Fernando had trouble falling asleep. When he did, he dreamed of men with painted faces dancing around the dead body of Gail Walker. The dancers carried rattlesnakes dangling from their mouths, writhing in the air like tentacles reaching out to grab him. He kept waking up and wiping the sweat from his face. Toward morning he finally fell into a deep sleep, only to be awakened by the sound of pots and pans clanking in the kitchen.

When his fog lifted, he realized Estelle was making breakfast in the kitchen. He waited until she finished her breakfast and packed her lunch. Then he heard the kitchen door open and close, followed by the sound of Estelle's Camry driving away. Not a word to him.

Fernando knew from experience that Estelle would cool off by the time she came home from work. She never stayed angry for long. One of her many virtues. He, on the other, liked to store up his anger, let it simmer for a while and then erupt in a burst of adrenaline.

He climbed out of bed and slipped into his jeans. He shuffled barefoot down the hall to the kitchen, where he poured himself a cup of coffee from the pot Estelle had left. When he finished the coffee, he shuffled back to the bedroom and finished getting dressed. By the time he returned to the kitchen and drank a second cup of coffee he was wide awake and had come to a decision. This morning he would take the package down to the Washington Avenue Station and hand it over to Manny. Let Manny worry about the video.

After a quick breakfast, Fernando went for a morning walk along Acequia Madre. Walking seemed to calm him better than anything else these days. Back in the day he smoked weed, but he no longer liked to put anything in his lungs. Walking and Modelo, those were his antidotes to stress and high blood pressure.

Later, after walking the length of Acequia Madre, he returned to his house and drank yet another cup of coffee. Then he went into the kitchen and took down the package from the shelf in the pantry. Should he re-tape it? More to the point, should he really give the package to Manny when he knew Russo and cowboy Wes would come calling sooner or later?

Then a plan occurred to him. He would take out the cell phone and give it to Manny, only the cell phone. That way he would save the package and the SpyFocus camera to give to Russo as a way to get the Film Collective off his back. He would just have to hope Russo couldn't download the video.

Leaving the package with the SpyFocus camera on his desk, he locked the house and took Jeff's iphone out to his Cherokee. Traffic was light this morning after rush hour had settled down, so he breezed down to the Paseo and around to Marcy Street. He turned left on Washington Avenue and parked in one of the visitor slots in the big parking lot. Not nearly as convenient as his former reserved parking place.

He didn't recognize the young woman at the front counter. Every time he came to the Washington Avenue Station he found a new person sitting at the counter. "Can I help you?" she asked, a moon-faced redhead with glasses.

"No, I know where I'm going," Fernando said and walked down the hallway to his old office.

Manny sat at his desk looking disgusted. The little man didn't say a word when Fernando walked in and sat in the chair across from the desk. Manny's desk was buried in a pile of papers and manila folders. Looked exactly like the last time Fernando was here, as if Manny hadn't done one damn thing to clear his paperwork. But Fernando couldn't talk. The desk had looked much the same when this had been his office, maybe worse.

"What's wrong with you?" Fernando asked.

"The Chief, as usual," Manny replied. "He's trying to rein in our investigation of the Film Collective boys. I'm trying to get a search warrant and bring them in for fingerprinting, but he's getting in my way. Tells me the film industry is too important to the city and state to tie it up in litigation. They're the number two source of income in the state, right after big oil. Santa Fe's become a second Hollywood, with direct flights to Los Angeles, and on and on."

"Money," Fernando said. "Money speaks louder than the law."

Manny nodded. "So what are you doing here?"

"Here's Jeff Walker's iphone," Fernando said, handing the cell phone to Manny. He wrote down the passcode on a slip of paper from his pocket notebook and passed it to Manny. "You can find the original of Jeff's video of the Hopi Snake Dance on this phone."

"Wait. How did you get this?" Manny asked.

"Gail Walker sent me a package containing Jeff's iphone and SpyFocus camera the day she was murdered," Fernando said. "I think she knew Max Russo and Wes Snyder from the Film Collective would be coming to her house to look for the Snake Dance video. Thing is, Russo and Snyder suspect I have the video now because when they raided her house and most likely murdered her they found a receipt for a UPS package addressed to me. They know she sent me something...why not the Snake Dance video?"

"Which in fact you do have," Manny pointed out.

"I know, and that's why they're already threatening me.

"You want back up? Security?" Manny asked.

Fernando shrugged. "I might. I'll let you know."

With that, Fernando turned and walked to the door of the office. Then he turned back to Manny. "Maybe you should show the video to the Chief. Might get him fired up to do something."

Manny laughed. "Or gross him out!"

7

On a whim Fernando decided to visit the Chief before leaving the Washington Avenue Station. So he went around the corner and down the corridor to the Chief's office. Mary, the Chief's secretary, greeted him in the central office. "Do you have an appointment?" she asked as he walked by, totally ignoring her. "Fernando?" she tried again.

Fernando walked through the open door into Chief Larry Stuart's office. Surprised, the Chief looked up from his terminal and said, "Fernando...to what do I owe this pleasure? Do you want to come back to work? We could use you."

Fernando laughed. "No, I'm afraid retirement has spoiled me."

The Chief smiled. "I hear you. I can't wait. I've already put in for retirement next year."

"You'll love it," Fernando said.

"Hey, but if you ever get bored and do want to come back, you'd be welcome with open arms," the Chief said. "You're the best damn detective we ever had. You and Antonio were our best team."

That was news coming from Larry Stuart, because the two of them had butted heads from the very beginning of Stuart's tenure at the SFPD. To Fernando Stuart was a newbie Anglo who knew next to nothing about Santa Fe. To the Chief Fernando was a smart-ass Chicano cop with a chip on his shoulder.

"Thanks, I appreciate that," Fernando said.

"What do you hear from Antonio?" the Chief asked.

"Not much," Fernando said. "He's helping his son run a ranch up in Colorado, somewhere near Alamosa. He kept his cabin in the Pecos in case he wanted to come back to visit, but I haven't heard from him since he left."

The Chief nodded. "So what's new with you?"

"I'm looking into the murder of Gail Walker, Jeff Walker's widow," Fernando said. "I think you know the situation. Apparently Jeff was paid to secretly film the Hopi Snake Dance but was killed or murdered driving back to Santa Fe. The people at Santa Fe Film Collective who paid him to do the job want the videotape of the dance. I think they killed Gail trying to find the film. Manny needs to bring them in for fingerprinting and a warrant to search the collective."

The Chief threw open his hands. "I know, but the mayor's the problem. He loves the film industry, wants Santa Fe to become an appendage of Hollywood. Sometimes I think it's personal with him—he just wants to hobnob with the stars."

Fernando nodded. That might be the first time he and the Chief had agreed on anything. "I can believe that."

"But you're right," the Chief continued. "We'll bring them in for fingerprinting this afternoon, both Russo and Snyder. The search warrant will have to wait until we have something more definite."

Fernando stood up but paused for a moment. "Here's another consideration. If the Hopis find out that an illicit video of the Snake Dance is circulating, the shit will literally hit the fan. It'll be a black eye for Santa Fe and anyone who had anything to do with the theft or the exploitation of the video, as well as those of us who didn't stop it. Heads will roll."

With that, Fernando turned and walked out of the office, leaving Stuart huddled at his desk looking worried, very worried.

"Is everything okay?" Mary asked as he walked by her desk.

Fernando didn't answer. Instead he walked down the hall and out the front door. Outside he saw a UPS truck drive down Washington Avenue and turn left on Palace. The truck reminded him of his earlier idea. Russo didn't know what was in the package, so why not re-tape the package containing only the SpyFocus camera and send it to the Film Collective? If they asked, he would tell them instead of opening the package he'd sent it on to them. Let them try to download the SpyFucus video. That might keep them busy and take the heat off him.

With that in mind, he drove directly home and carefully re-taped the package, trying to make it appear unopened. He did the best he could with the materials he had on hand in the kitchen and then drove back to the Paseo and around to West Alameda Street. He turned left and followed Alameda to Guadalupe, which took him to the downtown UPS store.

After dropping off the package, Fernando headed home. He drove around on the Paseo, but when he came to Acequia Madre Street the Devil got the better of him and he kept on going. He descended the hill and turned right immediately on Canyon Road, driving up to the El Farol parking lot.

He walked across Canyon Road to the venerable El Farol. The tables on the porch remained empty at this early hour. Inside he found a group of tourists at the bar arguing over where to go for dinner. One of the more lubricated males was talking loudly, saying he didn't want any more damn tacos, while everyone else in the group laughed. Very funny.

Fernando gave them the Evil Eye and walked into the restaurant part of El Farol, spotting Ruby sitting by her lonesome under the colorful flamenco mural on the wall. She waved as he approached.

"Good thing you're here, because I'm about ready to go tell those bozos in the bar to shut the fuck up," Ruby said.

"They'll be gone soon," Fernando replied. "They're arguing about where to go for dinner."

'I'll tell them where to go," Ruby said.

Fernando noticed Ruby's eyes were red. "Are you okay?" he asked.

"No, I'm not okay," Ruby said, pushing her long black hair out of her face. She took a handkerchief out of her purse and blew her nose. Then she sighed. "I'm holding a memorial for Gail at my pottery co-op. All the ladies want to do a remembrance of some sort. They all loved Gail and felt sorry for her. Same old story, good woman married to a worthless man."

Fernando laughed. "You say that about all men."

Ruby pointed to the doorway. "Here comes another one."

Fernando glanced behind him and saw Blaine Rogers and his new wife Tessa, who happened to be Ruby's younger sister, enter the room arguing with each other, as usual. Blaine stopped halfway through the door and turned back. "You want me to throw the loudmouths out?" he shouted to the bartender, who must have said no, because Blaine shrugged and walked into the dining area.

Not surprisingly, the loudmouths in the bar instantly quieted. Blaine had that effect on most people. At six-feet, four-inches tall and two hundred fifty pounds, Blaine intimidated nearly everyone. To make matters worse, Blaine had a nasty temper and usually registered somewhere fairly high on the obnoxious to half-crazed behavior spectrum.

Ruby shook her head when Blaine pulled up a chair at her table. She hadn't quite reconciled herself to Blaine marrying her younger sister. Tessa deserved better, after her first husband, Andy Dejon, turned out to be the world's worst philanderer.

"It's a little early to create a spectacle of yourself, even for you," Ruby said to Blaine, who slapped the table with the palm of his hand and yelled at the server, "Margarita, please! Make that two!"

Like Fernando, Tessa noticed that Ruby looked sad, unusual for Ruby. "What's wrong, sis? Have you been crying?"

Ruby waved her sister away. "Oh, I'll be okay. I'm organizing another memorial, this one for Gail Walker. Second one this season, right after Raoul Garcia. Before Raoul there was Fidel Rodriguez and Wayne Fontenot. Even Jimmy Mackey, my ex. Everyone's croaking. We're losing our entire generation."

"Not me," Tessa added. "I'm ten years younger, a different generation. Thank God!"

Ruby gave Tessa the Evil Eye.

"Don't start, Tess," Blaine warned.

Just then the server arrived with drinks for everyone, a Modelo draft for Fernando and margaritas for everyone else.

"Cheers!" Blaine said, raising his glass. "We're a lost generation— soon to be an extinct generation!"

Fernando raised his glass, forgetting all about telling Ruby the latest on the Hopi Snake Dance videos. Didn't seem like the appropriate time. They were saluting a soon-to-be-gone generation. Their generation!

8

Fernando awoke to a cloudy, windy day. A north wind came howling in over the Sangre de Cristo Mountains. More signs of the coming cold weather that always took him by surprise, arriving too abruptly. He didn't hear Estelle in the kitchen, so he figured she had already left for work. At least they had been talking again last night. Estelle seemed to have moved on from their latest argument.

He crawled out of bed and slipped into jeans and a flannel shirt he dug out of the closet. Then he shuffled barefoot down the hall to the kitchen, where he found a pot of coffee Estelle had left for him. He poured himself a cup and carried it into his study, since it was too damn windy to sit outside on the patio. While drinking his coffee, he booted up his laptop and searched for information on the Hopi Snake Dance. He was surprised to find pages of news stories, historical features, and opinion pieces on the mysterious dance. Some commentators called the dances 'grotesque' and 'primitive,' others referred to them as 'spiritual.'

Even more interesting to Fernando were the articles that concerned Hopis protesting against outsiders who used images and references to the Snake Dance for commercial purposes. He had no idea this problem was so widespread. One Arizona group in particular, the Smokis, actually mimicked the Hopi Snake Dance. For years the Smokis had put on an elaborate pageant ending with their own version of the Snake Dance, a violation of Hopi religion. Protests and lawsuits for cultural appropriation had followed many of these illegal uses, leaving a tangled web of litigation and counter litigation.

The more he read, the more outraged he became. He saw clearly that he had to prevent the Santa Fe Film Collective from using the video

Jeff Walker had illegally filmed. He left his study and searched the house for his cell phone. He found the iphone on his bed-stand and clicked the photo icon and then the Snake Dance video. He went to hit the delete button but stopped. Maybe he should keep the video for evidence, just in case Manny needs it. No one would see it on his iphone, so why not?

Just then a phone, their land line, rang in the kitchen. No one but scammers ever called on their land line, so he let it ring. He didn't know why they didn't get rid of the damn thing.

When the phone rang again, he picked up the receiver.

"Mister Lopez?" someone asked at the other end.

"Yes...who's this?"

"I'm calling on behalf of René Durand, the movie director...maybe you've heard of him or seen his work?" the voice asked.

"What a coincidence-" Fernando muttered out loud.

"Pardon?"

"Just talking to myself," Fernando said. "What do you want?"

"René wants to talk to you about the video of the Snake Dance that you have," the voice said.

Taken aback, Fernando wondered how René Durand knew he had the video...or even knew of the existence of the video. Had to be from Max Russo and the Santa Fe Film Collective. Maybe Durand was the client for whom the Santa Fe Film Collective was procuring the video.

"I can pick you up," the voice continued.

"No, I can drive myself," Fernando replied. The last thing he wanted was to be carted off somewhere by a stranger. "Where does he want to meet?"

"René is staying at the La Fonda Hotel. He says he will meet you there for lunch. How does Noon in La Plazuela sound to you?"

"Yeah," Fernando said and hung up, not sure if he would actually show. This turn of events further muddied the situation. Everyone wanted the damn video, not for any scientific or artistic reason, but to make money. Profit, pure and simple.

He had over an hour to kill, so he went back into his study and booted up his laptop again. This time he googled the director René Durand. Turned out the director was well known in France and across Europe for his pseudo-philosophical science fiction movies. He'd made movies about a global pandemic of untreatable Ebola virus; a shift in planetary orbits that created a weakening of gravity on earth; and a nuclear explosion that interrupted the space-time continuum and caused time to rewind. More recently Durand had been working on an unfinished movie version of *The Anomaly*, a blockbuster science fiction novel by the French writer Hervé Le Tellier. The novel followed several Parisian characters who became involved in a phenomenon known as the simulation hypothesis. On Air France flight 006 from Paris to New York their plane encounters a cumulonimbus supercell while landing at JFK International Airport. Three months later an exact duplicate of Air France flight 006 carrying exact duplicates of all passengers and crew on board the earlier flight appears in the sky over JFK and attempts to land, triggering mass confusion and panic. Weird stuff. He saw how half-naked Hopi dancers carrying rattlesnakes in their mouths might fit nicely in Durand's gallery of sensational images and narratives.

At a quarter till Noon Fernando closed his laptop and locked the house. He climbed into his Cherokee and drove around the Paseo to East Alameda Street. After plugging the meter, he walked up to Cathedral Place so he could enter La Fonda through its garage and hopefully avoid Fred Mondragon, who managed the hotel. Fred had banned Fernando from La Fonda because of his role in previous altercations involving several of his former clients. Try as he might, Fernando couldn't seem to convince Fred that it wasn't his fault that most of his clients tended to be somewhat volatile and not exactly law-abiding citizens.

Quietly and stealthily Fernando moved down the long hallway from the garage to La Fonda's lobby. He tried to keep his head down as he headed toward La Plazuela, off to his left.

"Fernando!" someone shouted from the front desk. He'd been spotted!

Fernando turned to find everyone at the front desk, including Fred Mondragon, staring at him. Fred wore his usual tan suit and a necktie as white as his hair. With his head lowered, the tiny old man leaned forward while clutching the counter as if holding on for dear life.

Caught red-handed, Fernando retraced his steps and walked up to the counter. "Don't worry, Fred. I'm here for a friendly meeting with the movie director René Durand. Won't be a problem, I promise."

Sighing, Fred nodded but said nothing for several awkward seconds. Then he said, "But you say that every time, Fernando."

"Trust me," Fernando said, turning away and walking toward the double glass doors of La Plazuela, hoping this meeting would be as friendly as he promised. Inside the patio restaurant he saw two men stand up at a table to greet him. One, a small 50-something man with a large nose in the middle of a thin, pinched face wore a plaid blue blazer and dark jeans. René Durand, no doubt. The other, tall and wiry, looked much younger and wore a maroon turtleneck over jeans.

Fernando walked across the flagstone floor and held out his hand. "Fernando Lopez."

"René Durand," the man in the blazer said, shaking Fernando's hand. "And zis is *mon secrétaire*, Roberto."

Roberto waved in a half-hearted, bored sort of way. His expression never changed. He wore a frown like some of the more arrogant types wore a smirk.

"Asseyez-vous, please," Durand said, pointing to the table.

Durand waited until Fernando sat down and then motioned for Roberto to begin his pitch.

"Mister Durand wants the video Jeff Walker shot of the Hopi Snake Dance," Roberto said. "He is willing to pay you fifty thousand dollars for the video...or a copy of the video."

Fernando smiled. "So that's your play. You think you can get the video from me for as little as fifty grand, instead of the two hundred grand Max Russo wants to charge you."

"*Si*...because as you see, Max Russo does not have za video," Durand added quickly.

"Well, I have news for you—I don't have it either," Fernando replied, not exactly truthfully.

The Frenchman lowered his head and looked positively crestfallen. "Zen we have a problem," he said softly.

"Let me ask you this," Fernando said. "Why do you want the video? What will you do with it? You know it's illegally obtained, right?"

Roberto nodded. "Mister Durand wants to use some clips in his new movie—"The Lower World"—now in production at Bonanza Creek Ranch, just south of Santa Fe. It's about what happens when the sun begins to dim and the world above turns into the world below, all dark. When that happens millions of snakes come up out of the ground, confused about where they belong, yes? And the only way to get them back in the ground is to do primitive magic. You know, like the Hopi Snake Dance, to return them to their rightful place in the rightful world below. Only the primitives know how to do this-"

Fernando held up his hand to stop Roberto. "We don't use the term 'primitives' here. The Hopi are anything but primitive. Call them Native Americans, or First Americans. You understand?"

Roberto frowned, pouting.

"*Dégueulasse,* the snakes, "Durand added when Roberto didn't speak.

"Whatever," Fernando said.

"You see, we think you do have a copy of the video," Roberto said finally. "In fact, we're sure you do."

Fernando shrugged. "Ask your friend Max Russo for a copy. He should have a package from Gail Walker arriving today."

Durand and Roberto looked at each other.

"So tell me more about your movie," Fernando said to Durand.

For the rest of an otherwise uneventful lunch, Fernando listened to Durand and Roberto talk about the plot of their movie—the fall into a dark sunless world of slithering snakes that only Hopi Snake Dancers could save from destruction.

When the three of them left La Fonda, an hour and a half later, Fred Mondragon was all smiles. He even waved from the front counter. At least for the time being, Fernando had earned his way back into Fred's good graces. He would see how long that would last.

9

Back at home Fernando went into his study and booted up his laptop again. This time he searched for any movie industry news about the shooting of 'The World Below.' He was surprised to find several mentions of Durand's new movie in industry newsletters and magazines. The city scenes, all filmed in or near Los Angeles, had been finished, according to these reports. The film crew had moved to New Mexico to shoot the Snake Dance scenes at Bonanza Creek Ranch south of Santa Fe and, rumor had it, at Walpi on Hopi's First Mesa.

While he scrolled through a few more mentions of the film he heard a vehicle pull into his driveway and stop. He checked the time. Too early for Estelle to be coming home from work.

Fernando closed his laptop and walked into the kitchen. From the kitchen window he saw a tan panel truck parked at the end of his driveway. He didn't recognize the truck.

He waited, but the truck didn't move. It just sat there, out of place and to Fernando ominous. He didn't like unknown vehicles parked in his driveway. What the hell did they want?

He quickly went into his study to get his Smith & Wesson, which he strapped on and then walked out of the kitchen door into the driveway. He saw a logo on the side of the panel truck: a circle with a pistol inside and 'City Different Security' printed underneath in red letters. He'd never heard of 'City Different Security.' What did they want with him?

Coming closer, he spotted only one person in the truck, a man sitting in the driver's seat. A big man, with huge shoulders and a Los Angeles Dodgers baseball cap pulled down almost over his eyes. The big gorilla buzzed down his side window as Fernando approached.

"Can I help you?" Fernando asked, noticing the size of the man. This guy could be trouble. Physically, Max Russo and Wes Snyder didn't pose much of a problem, and neither did René Durand and his secretary Roberto. This guy was a different story entirely.

The big guy glared at him from the front seat of the panel truck. "Yeah, I'm here to pick up the Snake Dance video. Max Russo sent me."

"So who are you?" Fernando asked.

"I'm with City Different Security," the big man said. "We provide security for the Santa Fe Film Collective on all their movie sets and anywhere else they need it. Name's Cody."

"Cody," Fernando repeated, always amused by what he considered cowboy names. Anglos loved them some cowboy names. "I don't have the video. I told René Durand the same thing."

"You'd be wise to stay away from René Durand!" Cody snapped. "He has nothing to do with this transaction. We paid for the video and we intend to get it. You understand?"

"I sent the video to Max Russo yesterday," Fernando continued, ignoring Cody's comment about Durand. "He should get it in the mail today."

"You mean this?" Cody said. He reached over to the passenger's seat and grabbed the package containing the SpyFocus camera Fernando had re-taped and mailed to the Santa Fe Film Collective yesterday.

Cody tossed the empty package out of the window. It landed at Fernando's feet. No camera.

Fernando frowned. He didn't like this guy's attitude, not one bit. "Detective Manny Alvarez at the Santa Fe Police Department has Walker's iphone, if that's what you're looking for. I'm sure he'd be more than happy to share it with you," he said sarcastically.

Cody glared at him. "Come on, Lopez, you must have made a copy of the video for yourself. If not, then have Alvarez send you a copy. Doesn't matter to me either way. Just so I get a copy."

"Well, I'm sure you know where the Washington Avenue Police Station is located, " Fernando said as calmly as possible. "You've probably spent some time there, right?"

"I'll give you forty-eight hours," Cody said, ignoring Fernando's comment. "I'll be back to pick it up. Or else there will be consequences."

Fernando approached the open window, resting his hands on the door. He stared at Cody. "You come any closer to my house and I'll kill you," he said in the coldest, matter-of-fact voice he could muster.

"Forty-eight hours," Cody said and threw his panel truck in reverse. He backed up a few feet, and sped off down the driveway onto Acequia Madre, leaving Fernando in a cloud of dust.

Cursing, Fernando watched the panel truck disappear on Acequia Madre. He didn't take kindly to punks like Cody giving him orders. Never had.

Fernando walked into the house and immediately called Manny.

"Good thing you called, I have some news," Manny said. "Russo and Snyder came in for fingerprinting yesterday. They're clean. Forensics didn't find their fingerprints at Gail Walker's house."

"Yeah, well I have another candidate, a guy by the name of Cody who works for an outfit called City Different Security," Fernando said. "He just stopped by wanting the video of the Snake Dance and threatening me if he didn't get it."

"Cody Hunt," Manny said. "Watch out for him. He's been involved in a number of fights and brawls that landed him in jail. He's dangerous, especially when he's been drinking."

"Great...just what I wanted to hear."

"I hope you're not planning to give him a copy of the video," Manny continued. "It's illegal to secretly record a tribal dance that's closed to the public. The Tribal Police will be up in arms if they find out."

"Don't worry, I'm not giving the sonofabitch anything," Fernando said. "But Max Russo's not the only one asking me for a copy of the video. René Durand, the movie director who contracted with the Santa Fe Film Collective to shoot the video, offered me fifty thousand dollars for a copy. He figures he can get it from me cheaper than what the Film Collective wants to charge him."

"That's news to me," Manny said. "Who's Durand? What's his interest in the video?"

Fernando explained that Durand was shooting a movie, 'The Lower World,' at Bonanza Creek Ranch and wanted to include a clip or two of the Hopi Snake Dance Video.

"Why the Hopi Snake Dance, I don't get it," Manny said.

Fernando summarized the movie's plot, as far as he knew it. "Only the Snake Dancers can get the snakes to go back to where they belong—in the world below," Fernando said.

"What horseshit!" Manny responded.

"Tell me about it," Fernando agreed. "Same old apocalyptic crap."

"Well...I better pay a visit to the Santa Fe Film Collective," Manny said. "Maybe even go out to 'The Lower World' film set at Bonanza Creek Ranch. That's just south of Santa Fe, a few miles off Interstate twenty-five. I might even call Jody Williams to give her a head's up."

"Good idea," Fernando said. He knew Jody Williams, the Santa Fe County Sheriff, from past cases when he was a Santa Fe Police Detective and then a private investigator. A damn fine cop.

"What do you think? You wanna come with me to Bonanza Creek Ranch?" Manny asked.

"Why not," Fernando replied.

"Okay, meet me down here at the station, say four o'clock."

10

Nearing Picture Rock on Highway 14 Manny pulled over to pee. He climbed out of the cruiser and left Fernando sitting in the front passenger's seat admiring the high mountain scenery on the road they called the Turquoise Trail: green sagebrush grasslands and triangular hills pock-marked by piñon and gnarly juniper trees, sparkling in the bright New Mexico sunshine. They'd had to take Highway 14, much slower than I-25 after the southbound lane of the interstate had been shut down because of a fatal accident on the always dangerous La Bajada Hill. Speed kills, just like the saying goes. Every year some of the crazy hotshots in the Santa Fe/Albuquerque area tried going down La Bajada at a hundred miles an hour or more and ended up squashed road kill on the highway. So it goes.

Finished, Manny walked back to the cruiser zipping up his pants and scooted into the driver's seat. He noticed Fernando staring at him. "I have a prostate problem. I have to pee every two hours."

Fernando laughed. "Join the club. How old are you anyway?"

"Forty-seven," Manny replied, pulling back out on Highway 14.

Just before Picture Rock Manny turned right on Bonanza Creek Road and zig-zagged north, west, and then north again. "The only thing I know about Bonanza Creek Ranch is what happened on the Rust movie set, where Alex Baldwin accidentally shot the cinematographer."

Fernando nodded. "Never been there." The only experience he had with movie people was during his Taos Vendetta case. He wasn't very impressed. Bunch of primadonnas.

Minutes later Manny turned off on the road to Bonanza Creek Ranch. They came to a post fence with an arched ranch gate entrance without the gate, only the high lonesome frame above the dirt road. Manny followed the curving road into the ranch, a sprawling property of rocky hills surrounded by a sea of prairie with a scattering of trees here and there. Soon the various movie sets came into view: the Western Town Set, the Pond House Set, the Astro Barn Set, and the Mountain Cabin Set, all clearly marked by road signs.

Up ahead they saw an unmarked building where a group of people had gathered, sitting at picnic tables under the shade of a sizeable awning. Manny parked in a grassy parking area where all the other cars and trucks were parked. Everyone stopped talking and watched Manny and Fernando climb out of the cruiser and walk over to the crowd of onlookers.

Fernando followed Manny over to a tall, well-toned young man wearing a western shirt and bolo tie who held a clipboard in his hand. He looked like an actor, or maybe a stunt man.

"Hello, I'm looking for the 'Lower World' movie set," Manny said in a friendly tone of voice. "Do you know where I can find it?"

"Yessir, it's over on the Mountain Cabin Set," he replied, pointing down the road to the left. "Everything all right? Nobody wanted by the law, I hope."

"Not at the moment," Manny said, not very reassuringly.

The young man smiled but seemed confused by Manny's response. Finally he nodded, moving back away from Manny.

"Much obliged," Fernando said to the young man and then followed Manny back to the cruiser.

Without speaking, Manny fired up the cruiser and headed down the road. He came quickly to an intersection where the road diverged to the different movie sets. He turned left toward the Mountain Cabin Set.

They saw trailers up ahead, four of them parked around a central tent. Crew members unloaded cameras, props, and other equipment from two of the trailers. Other crew members, both men and women, carried cameras and other equipment up a narrow trail to the rocky top of an adjacent mesa. They seemed to be preparing for an evening or night shoot.

Manny parked out of the way, behind the trailers, and then climbed out of the cruiser and slammed the door.

Fernando followed. He looked around, spotting the so-called mountain cabin off to the side of the road. Erected in front of a stand of trees, the L-shaped cabin had a stone fireplace at one end. It looked to be constructed of rough-cut lumber stained a deep brown to resemble logs. Very small, but at least from a distance, it looked more or less authentic.

Fernando turned his attention to Manny, who'd gone over to the group of people gathered at the tent. He'd found René Durand and his secretary, Roberto. Durand was pointing to the top of the mesa.

Joining them, Fernando eased up behind Manny and let him do the talking. The ever dapper Durand, still wearing his suit, seemed irritated by the appearance of Manny and Fernando. He denied knowing anything about the murder of Gail Walker or the whereabouts of the video her husband had made of the Hopi Snake Dance. He did acknowledge that he had contracted with the Santa Fe Film Collective to obtain the video.

Manny nodded but didn't tell Durand he had a copy of the video of the Snake Dance.

Finally Durand turned to Fernando and asked, "What about you... do you have video?"

"No," he said, shaking his head, which was marginally true. He had a copy, not the original video.

Durand looked at his watch. "We shoot in one hour, Roberto."

"Yeah, I have to get busy," Roberto said to Manny and Fernando. "We start shooting at dusk, as soon as it starts to get dark. If you want to take a look at the set, it's up on the mesa. We modeled the set on what we found in the famous 1913 video that's in the Library of Congress. The set includes the wall of an adobe building and a shallow indentation of a kiva. The dancing area has been graded and flattened for the dancers. You can go up and see for yourself."

Manny frowned, clearly troubled by what Roberto had just said. "Are you sure you really want to do this?"

"What do you mean?" Roberto asked, impatient to get started on his preparations for the shoot. Wearing jeans, a T-shirt, and hiking boots, he was ready to get to work on the mesa.

"What I mean is that this is cultural appropriation," Manny replied. "You're appropriating, in what some would say a disrespectful manner, a sacred tradition in Hopi culture. While there's no specific law to prevent you from staging a Hopi Snake Dance, it certainly is cultural appropriation for the sole purpose of making money. That's likely a violation of intellectual property rights."

Roberto shook his head. "We're just making entertainment. What's the problem with that?"

Manny glared at Roberto. "That doesn't excuse you from the norms of cultural respect and decency. What you're doing—emphasizing the sensational aspects of the Snake Dance—will just reinforce the worst stereotypes of Hopi and other Native American religious ceremonies."

"And it's bad juju," Fernando added, remembering what Ruby and Blaine had said about a curse.

Roberto sighed. "Well, let's just agree to disagree. Anyway, help yourself to a look at our set. In fact, you're welcome to stick around until we start filming. You might change your mind if you see René at work. He's very artistic. A genius, if you really want to know."

"You wanna take a look?" Manny asked Fernando after Roberto had walked away.

"Why not...since we're here?"

"Why not," Manny repeated and headed up the narrow trail, with Fernando following a few steps behind.

On their way up the steep trail they were passed by crew members carrying props and equipment up the trail. One burly man in a sweat suit carried an armful of drums that looked authentic but probably weren't. The next crew member who passed them carried an armful of rubber snakes dangling every which way from his arms. Fernando did a double take. Rubber snakes?

Manny cursed when he saw the rubber snakes. Turning to Fernando, he said, "Look at that! Can you believe it? Fucking rubber snakes! Toys!"

No words adequately described Fernando's disgust. "A real mockery," he replied finally, the best he could come up with at the moment.

They trudged up to the top of the mesa, entering a flat plaza area that would be used by the snake dancers. At the far end of the mesa the stage setting had been erected: a canvas backdrop attached to a wooden frame that depicted an adobe structure with an open door. Images of animal skins and red chile ristras had been painted on the canvas. Off to both sides of the canvas building, a real adobe wall had been added for a touch of realism. Not only for show, the waist-high adobe wall could be used for sitting, as they saw walking across the plaza. Several crew members sat on the wall taking a break from their work.

"Look at this," Fernando said, pointing to a two-foot deep circle that served as a kiva on the set. Stones had been placed around the circumference of the circle. One of the crew members had callously, cynically tossed a couple of rubber snakes into the mock kiva; one of the discarded snakes had a cigarette stuck in its open mouth for some kind of sick joke. All the other rubber snakes had been tossed on the ground near an opening in the canvas that served as a door to the backstage area, so to speak, where lots of cameras and equipment were stored, ready to be used later that afternoon when shooting would begin.

"Very funny," Manny said. "What a fucking desecration. I've seen enough, let's get the hell out of here."

After one last look, Fernando turned and headed back down the trail. Manny followed, making comments as he walked. His comments were not flattering to the set or the movie.

Back at the tent Durand and Roberto were already making final preparations for the shoot, giving directions to the camera crew and the actors, all of whom were dressed in a movie version of Hopis: war paint smeared on their faces and naked chests, animal skins hanging from leather breeches, and feathers attached everywhere. Ready to mimic the famous Hopi Snake Dance.

Fernando burst out laughing when he saw them. The actors were all Anglo or Hispanic. He couldn't identity a Native American among them. Equity actors from Santa Fe and Albuquerque.

Manny was so angry he cursed and then stormed away without saying a word to anyone.

Seeing Fernando, Roberto came over carrying a clipboard. "So what did you think?"

Fernando laughed again. He shook his head. Finally he said, "I think it's an abomination."

Roberto's smile faded. "Well...each to his own. René is a genius. You will see his magic when the film is released."

"I hope the film is never released," Fernando said.

Roberto frowned but said nothing.

Fernando followed Manny through the crowd. He noticed the sun had set in the western sky, leaving streaks of red and purple on the horizon. Dusk would arrive soon and the filming would begin.

When he reached the cruiser he found Manny leaning against the hood, waiting for him. Manny pointed to the picnic tables where none other than Cody stood, glaring at them.

"Looks like trouble," Fernando said.

"He always is," Manny added.

The streetlights flashed on as Fernando turned onto Acequia Madre Street. He pulled into his driveway and sat in the Cherokee for a few minutes brooding. He'd come away from Bonanza Creek Ranch with an unsettled feeling, with unresolved issues that gnawed at him. The filming of the Snake Dance was clearly an insult to the Hopi, disrespectful to say the least, but it wasn't clear to him—or to Manny for that matter—that it broke any of the existing laws. Manny mentioned cultural appropriation and violation of intellectual property rights, but those issues would have to be sorted out in a complicated and very expensive litigation. Fernando doubted the Hopi Tribe or the State of Arizona would be willing to fund such expensive litigation with uncertain results, win or lose.

Climbing out of the Cherokee, Fernando noticed that Estelle's Camry wasn't parked in its usual spot in front of the garage. Must be working late, he figured. As soon as he walked into the kitchen he grabbed a Modelo out of the refrigerator and sat down at the kitchen table. The cold Modelo never tasted better, so he drank it quickly and opened another. Halfway through the second Modelo his cell phone pinged on the kitchen table. He read the message from Estelle: "Staff dinner tonight after Board of Directors meeting. Be home late, between nine and ten o'clock. Sorry I won't be there for dinner. Love, Estelle."

That further disrupted Fernando's day, adding to the disarray. Now he was at loose ends. Without his routine he felt unmoored, lost in space. He'd been diagnosed as obsessive-compulsive a few years back by a shrink Estelle insisted he make an appointment with, but his OCD only reared its head in crazy moments like this. Anyway, wasn't everyone obsessive-compulsive when they reached a certain age? All the old timers he knew.

He needed a plan. A plan would bring a semblance of order to an otherwise amorphous day. He walked outside to the patio and checked the sky. Dusk already. That meant the filming would begin soon on 'The Lower World' movie at Bonanza Creek Ranch. Why not drive back down and watch how the cast and crew are filming the movie? That might help him make up his mind about the movie and its cultural appropriation.

Feeling better now that he had a plan of sorts, Fernando quickly ate a bowl of leftover green chile stew with corn tortillas and hit the road. He decided to take Interstate-25, the fastest route, even though he didn't like driving at high speeds in the dark. Too many animals, both human and otherwise, likely to dart across the road in front of oncoming vehicles.

To compensate for the limited night vision, he drove a good ten miles an hour below the speed limit. After he cleared the outskirts of Santa Fe, he saw a three-quarters moon hanging in the sky over the hills southeast of the city. He turned left onto Bonanza Creek Road and plunged into piñon-spotted hills criss-crossed by bone dry arroyos. Occasionally the moonlight would strike the piñon branches just right to make them glow silver in the darkness, like apparitions or ghosts stalking the mesa, looking to cause mischief.

The wooden gate erected over the entrance to Bonanza Creek Ranch appeared in his headlights as Fernando crossed over Alamo Creek. He slowed down and turned into the driveway. Up ahead he saw a few dim lights at the office and an eerie yellow glow hovering over the mesa where Reñe Durand's film was being shot. Looked like the mesa was glowing from the inside, like a gigantic lantern... or as if a UFO was hovering overhead, beaming down a yellow ray on the mesa.

He drove up behind the trailers and parked in the shadows, out of sight. All the action was on the mesa, where he could hear both drumming and chanting. Climbing out of the Cherokee, he paused for a moment to look around. He saw no one in the shadows, so he walked to the dirt trail leading to the top of the mesa. The singing grew louder as he climbed the trail. As he approached the top, he spotted a ledge of rock to the left of the trail from where he could see over the lip of the mesa without being seen. At least he hoped he couldn't be seen. He had no idea how he would be received if someone noticed him spying on the shoot.

Fernando studied the plaza area, illuminated by a roaring bonfire and torches placed strategically around all sides of the plaza area that together produced a sickly yellow glow. He hated to admit it, but from his vantage point the stone pueblo painted on the canvas looked damned near real. The lighting and special effects were stunning, very creative. Moments later five or six snake dancers in costume danced around and through the smoke from the bonfire, chanting "Ay-ya…Ay-ya…Ay-ya."

While Fernando watched, the dancers circled around the snake pit and then dipped down, one at a time, pulling rubber snakes out of the pit. The dancers first stroked the snakes as if trying to put them asleep and then stuffed the rubber snakes in their mouths, clenching the rubber props with their teeth. As they danced they shook their heads, flopping the rubber snakes from side to side, like dogs playing with a rubber toy. Fernando bit his tongue, trying not to laugh at the spectacle that was not only grotesque and sensational, but downright absurd, given the fact that the snakes were rubberized toys.

Finally he couldn't control himself. He placed his hand over his mouth to muffle his laughter but with limited effect. Someone on the mesa heard him chuckling and started down the trail. Fernando saw a tall, wiry man with broad shoulders holding a clipboard in his hands. Though the tall man's face was lost in the dark and the smoke from the fire, Fernando knew instinctively who he was: Roberto, René Durand's secretary.

"What are you doing here? Are you spying on us?" Roberto barked, not bothering to control his hostility.

"That's funny," Fernando said, "after the spying you paid for in order to get a stolen video of the Snake Dance."

Roberto failed to see the humor. His right hand suddenly lashed out with the clipboard. Before Fernando could duck, the edge of the clipboard slashed across his forehead. The blow sent him reeling to his right. Stumbling, he lost his balance and fell off the rocky ledge. He crash-landed on his back, sliding down the hillside over rocks and cactus and other sharp objects that pierced his clothing and punctured his skin. He yelped out in pain as he came to rest against a small boulder that came out of nowhere to smack the back of his head.

Dizzy and in a great deal of pain, Fernando lay quietly for a few moments trying to gather his wits. The pain helped him focus. He felt the pinpricks and scratches on his back and legs. And something else, a wetness on his face. He touched his face and felt blood running down both cheeks and into his eyes, blood everywhere. Cursing, he tried to get to his feet but fell again. Finally he got on his hands and knees and crawled down the hill until he found the trail. He looked around to make sure Roberto was nowhere in sight. Then he fought his balance to get to his feet. Once he could stand without falling, he carefully shuffled down the trail to the nearest trailer, where he leaned against the aluminum siding to rest. He kept trying to wipe the blood out of his eyes with his shirtsleeve with limited effect.

Blinded by blood, he staggered over to his Cherokee and opened the rear compartment where he kept a supply of bottled water. He twisted the cap off one of the bottles and poured it over his face, wiping again with his shirtsleeve. Then he took the kerchief he always carried in his rear pocket and tied it tight around his forehead to stop the bleeding.

He heard Roberto coming down the trail looking for him. "Lopez? Lopez? Where are you?"

Time to get the hell out of here. Feeling a burst of adrenalin, he opened the driver's door of the Cherokee and crawled in. He fumbled with his keys for a few moments, before managing to start the big engine. He saw Roberto straight ahead when he switched on his headlights. Overcome by a blind rage, Fernando stomped down hard on the accelerator. The Cherokee spun to the left, then caught and headed directly for Roberto. Fernando wanted nothing more than to hit the sonofabitch and send him flying ass over head into the rocks.

Roberto jumped a moment too late. The Cherokee caught his arm and sent him spinning into the bushes with a look of abject horror on his face. The image of that face cheered Fernando temporarily,

After clipping Roberto, the Cherokee careened back onto the road, which Fernando followed out to Bonanza Creek Road and Interstate-25. He had to drive slowly because blood kept getting into his eyes. He wanted to avoid the Christus Saint Vincent Emergency Room because he knew from experience he would be there all night if he stepped foot in that damn place. So he headed for Santa Fe Urgent Care on Saint Michael's Drive, which he'd used before.

Squinting and still wiping blood out of his eyes with his shirtsleeve, he plodded along the highway to the Saint Francis Drive Exit. When he finally reached the Urgent Care on Saint Michael's Drive, he parked right in front in a handicapped parking space and managed to crawl out of the Cherokee.

Wobbling, he shuffled through the automatic doors and staggered into the waiting room. Everyone in the room stared at him, including the intake people at the front counter. At that moment he realized how macabre he must look, with a bleeding headband wrapped around his head and blood splattered all over his shirt and jeans, not to mention his face. The walking dead had nothing on him.

The Grim Reaper arriveth!

"Jesus!" one of the people sitting in the waiting room exclaimed. "What happened to him?"

Instantly a nurse came racing around the corner with a wheelchair. She circled around behind him and pushed the chair up against his legs with such force that he fell backwards into the chair.

"Hang on!" she said, but Fernando was already out cold.

12

Fernando awoke with an IV dripping into his arms, EKG wires pasted all over his chest, and a bad attitude. What the fuck? They'd kidnapped him like a damn emergency room.

A monitor beeped somewhere behind him. Moments later a young nurse entered his room and turned the beeper off. "You might feel a little pull here," she said, pulling off the EKG wires one at a time.

He was wide awake now and ready to go. Were they ready to let him go—that was the question.

"We called your wife, thinking she might want to come get you," the nurse said, smiling. "She said, I quote, 'tell him I don't care if he ever comes home.'"

Yep, that sounded like his Estelle, as feisty as ever. Basically telling him to go to hell.

"Ouch," Fernando yelped, after the young nurse ripped a patch of hair off his bare chest.

"Sorry," the nurse said, winking at him. "Sounds like you've been a bad boy lately."

"You too?" Fernando asked.

She smiled and made a face. "Well, you're lucky. Your CT-scan showed only a mild concussion, and the doc was able to stitch the gash in your forehead with disappearing stitches."

"Thing is, I need to get out of here," Fernando said.

She raised her hand. "I'm here to take out the IV—it's just a matter of waiting for your discharge orders."

She removed the IV and left him. An hour later a doc came into his room, a young man with a bald head and a long white coat, his only distinguishing features. He told Fernando the exact same thing the nurse told him and then left. Another hour later the nurse came back in with his discharge papers, which he signed quickly and jumped up, ready to roll.

Before he could reach the door, the nurse grabbed a wheelchair in the hallway and said, "Let's get you out of here."

Fernando looked down at the wheelchair and frowned. "I'm a bad boy, remember," he said and marched out of the room, down the long hallway, and out of the automatic doors without once looking back.

Outside, he stopped for a moment, having forgotten where he parked the Cherokee. Fortunately he spotted the Cherokee parked crookedly in a handicapped space, an indication of his distress when he first arrived.

Fernando climbed gingerly into the Cherokee and sat back for a moment. His entire body had begun to ache, his muscles stiffen. He could tell that by tomorrow morning he would be in a lot of pain.

He fired the big engine and headed home. By the time he turned into his driveway on Acequia Madre it was past Midnight, the end of an exhausting day. But at least he'd come to a decision. He would do everything he could to prevent 'The Lower World' from ever being filmed and released. What that would entail he had no idea at the moment, none whatsoever

He parked alongside Estelle's Camry and then walked up to the dark house. Estelle had not only not waited up for him, she hadn't even left a light on. Another bad sign.

He knew she would be pissed. Better not to wake her. So as quietly as possible, Fernando opened the kitchen door and crept inside. He turned on the small light above the stove for just enough light to see what he was doing.

After placing his Urgent Care papers on the kitchen table, he took off his shoes and stripped down to his underwear. He wadded up his bloody shirt and jeans and stuffed them in the kitchen garbage can under a layer of trash. He didn't want Estelle to see how much blood he'd lost.

Next he tip-toed down the hallway to their bedroom and, as quietly as possible, crawled into bed beside Estelle. He breathed a sigh of relief when she didn't stir. But as soon as he closed his eyes, she turned her head slightly toward him and said, "I don't want to hear."

Exhausted, he fell into a sleep so deep that he felt like he'd entered the land of the dead. No dreams, no nightmares, just nothingness black and endless. And when he awoke, he felt like he'd just returned from the land of the dead. His entire body was sore from his fall: his back, his shoulders, his legs. Not to mention the gash on his forehead where Roberto had clobbered him with a clipboard. Everything.

Lying in bed, he hoped Estelle had already gone to work. He didn't have the strength to face her this morning.

No such luck. He heard noises from their kitchen, the clank of the coffee pot, their kitchen faucet, and a chair scraping the floor. He struggled to get out of bed, shuffling slowly into the bathroom where he held his head under the sink faucet and then toweled off, careful to not disturb the bandage on his forehead. He pulled on a clean pair of jeans and a T-shirt from his dresser drawer and then headed down the hallway to face the music.

Estelle sat at the kitchen table with her arms crossed. The discharge papers he'd received at the Urgent Care were spread out on the table before her, along with a cup of coffee.

"I see you had quite a night," Estelle said.

"I'm fine," he replied.

"Well, you don't look fine," Estelle said. "A concussion and fifteen stitches? What happened to you?"

Fernando shrugged. "I took a nasty fall...fell down from the top of a hill in the dark. My own clumsiness," he said, forcing himself to laugh. A half-truth was better than no truth, he figured.

He could tell Estelle didn't believe him by her silence. She continued to stare at him until finally she raised her hand. "Enough. I don't want to hear any more. I'm off to work."

With that, Estelle stood and grabbed her lunch bag on her way out of the house. As she opened the door to leave, she turned to Fernando and said, "I hope you're home for dinner tonight, so we can eat together like normal people."

Fernando watched her walk to her Camry and drive off. Normal people? Did they know any normal people? He had to wonder.

13

Once Estelle left for work, Fernando got down to carrying out his plan for the day: getting rid of the aches and pains that made it difficult to do anything, especially walk. He did a few light exercises and then walked around the house between cups of coffee to loosen his muscles. That helped, as did the Advil he popped. The doc at Urgent care had given him a prescription for opioids, but he hadn't stopped at the pharmacy to fill it. He preferred to avoid opioids, if at all possible. Advil and Modelo usually worked for him.

The bandage on his forehead itched nonstop, driving him crazy. When he looked in the mirror he couldn't believe the size of the damn bandage. It looked like he'd just had brain surgery or something equally horrific. So, determined, he carefully removed the bandage, examined his stitches, and replaced the monstrous bandage with a regular sized Band Aid, which almost but not quite covered the nasty wound. Only a little red showed. He could live with that. Maybe it would even elicit some sympathy from Estelle and others.

Payback, on the other hand, would have to wait until the opportunity presented itself. He had a little something he wanted to give to that sonofabitch Roberto. All in good time.

At the moment he wanted to know what the chances were that a court order, or legal action of some sort, could stop René Durand from using—or stealing—the Hopi Snake Dance for his movie. Since Raoul Garcia had died, he didn't have a friendly lawyer whose advice he respected. That meant he would have to visit Steve Chabot, the Santa

Fe County District Attorney. He didn't particularly like Chabot. They'd had their differences back when Fernando worked as lead detective at the Santa Fe Police Department, but what choice did he have?

So Fernando called Chabot's office and made a one o'clock appointment that afternoon, thanks to Chabot's secretary Ruth Alarid, who happened to be one of Estelle's best friends.

Since he had time to kill, Fernando went for a long walk on Acequia Madre Street, which loosened his tight muscles. By the time he returned home his legs felt almost pain free. Almost. After a light lunch he headed downtown to Chabot's office on Sandoval Street. The small parking lot was full, so he had to park on the street and plug the meter.

Ruth greeted him as he walked into the office. "Fernando Lopez, I didn't know you and Steve were on talking terms," she said, laughing.

Fernando laughed too. Sort of. "Time to let bygones be bygones, Ruth. I learned that from Estelle. She forgives me for all of my infractions."

"Hah! I bet that keeps her busy," Ruth joked. "She tells me about some of your cases."

That was news to Fernando. He didn't like his work as a fixer to get around. Better to keep it private. On the down-low.

Just then the door to Chabot's office opened and a smiling Steve Chabot greeted Fernando. "Come on back," Chabot said cheerfully.

Fernando was a bit surprised by Steve Chabot's cordiality. Must have something to do with Fernando's role in finding his son Chris' killer in their recent Peyote Circle case.

He followed Chabot into his office, a tidy mahogany-laden office that looked expensive, just like Steve Chabot himself, who always wore a three-piece suit and tie, which matched his well-coiffed and tanned appearance. Chabot looked much younger than his age, late fifties.

Chabot pointed to two chairs facing each other on an oriental rug. Fernando sat in the chair nearest the window, always appreciative of the light.

"So what's up, Fernando? Thanks again for what you did for Chris. I appreciate that," Chabot said. "By the way, what did you do to your forehead? Looks swollen."

"I didn't duck fast enough," Fernando said, not wanting to explain.

Chabot laughed. "I won't ask for the details."

Fernando nodded. "Anyway, I have a legal question for you. It concerns a movie being filmed at Bonanza Creek Ranch that intends to use a secret recording of the Hopi Snake Dance."

"Really?" Chabot replied.

"Did you see the story in the *Independent* about the death of Jeff Walker, a Santa Fe photographer who'd run off the road coming back from a dance on the Hopi Reservation?"

"I saw it, yes."

Fernando went on to explain that Walker had surreptitiously videotaped the Hopi Snake Dance for the Santa Fe Film Collective, which intended to sell the videotape to the French director René Durand. He described how Durand intended to use the videotape in the film he was shooting at Bonanza Creek Ranch, where his film production was staging a re-enactment of the Snake Dance with actors and fake scenery.

"This is clearly cultural appropriation and a mockery of an important part of Hopi culture," Fernando pointed out. "My question is this: can we get a court order to stop the appropriation? Stop the violation?"

Chabot shook his head sadly. "I wish it were that simple. The law here is fuzzy, for lack of a better word. You'd first have to have standing and then be able to show how you would be damaged if this nonsense were allowed to continue. Cultural appropriation is very difficult to prove— and very expensive. Same with a violation of intellectual property."

Fernando nodded. He expected this, but he hoped there was some other way to proceed.

"Thing is, we do this all the time," Chabot continued. "For example in our Santa Fe Fiesta pageants and parades. We let Anglos play Hispanics and Native Americans...and vice versa. They perform these roles in order to celebrate and commemorate our history."

"But this use is based on profit—to make money at the box office," Fernando responded. "Because these images are sensational—and if taken out of context, grossly primitive."

"Yes, but the director will say the use is artistic, that copyright protects artistic license," Chabot said. "Let me give you a more direct example. Have you heard of the Smokis?"

"Yes," Fernando admitted.

"They're a group of white men who have been performing a version of the Hopi Snake Dance since the 1930s, I believe," Chabot continued. "Every year the Hopis and even the Zuñis protest at the dances, but neither of the tribes have been able to stop the dances in court."

Fernando nodded, trying to think. There must be a way, a different angle.

"So to answer your question, no, I wouldn't ask a judge for a court order to stop the filming," Chabot said. "The Hopi would have to come to me and request that I stop it at least temporarily while a judge weighs the legal issues, but even if they did, I think it would be a lost cause."

Fernando did not respond. He was out of ideas.

"I'm sorry, Fernando," Chabot said. "I agree with you that it's an abomination...one of many allowed these days, if you ask me. What you could do is to work with the director and try to get him to tone down his use, minimize it, or whatever you could convince him to do—or not do."

"Yeah...okay," Fernando said.

"Otherwise, I just don't know...." Chabot said.

After a long silence, Fernando replied, "I guess I'll just have to find another way then."

"What do you mean?"

Fernando didn't answer because he didn't know or have an answer. Instead, he stood and walked out of Chabot's office.

He was a fixer. He would find another way.

14

Santa Fe County Sheriff Jodie Williams called Fernando that evening. He'd just finished their after dinner cleanup when his cell phone rang. When he saw who was calling, he stepped outside to their patio so Estelle couldn't hear. He expected bad news. He wasn't disappointed.

"Fernando, what the hell's going on down there at Bonanza Creek Ranch?" Jodie asked, sounding angrier than she usually sounded. "Manny just called and told he a bunch of yahoos were making a movie about the Hopi Snake Dance. Don't they know anything about tribal law and customs?"

"Apparently not," Fernando said. "Or if they do, they're willing to disregard it to make a few bucks."

"Not only that, but Manny tells me the director is French. Is that even possible? French?"

Fernando laughed. "I'm afraid so, his name's René Durand. He makes all these apocalyptic, end-of-the-world movies."

"Well, he's gonna get an apocalypse, all right. Manny called the Hopi tribal office and told the Governor."

That got Fernando's attention. "Oh shit! I was hoping he wouldn't. Now all hell's gonna break loose."

"That's why I'm calling," Jodie said. "This is Santa Fe County, my jurisdiction. I have to deal with this crazy shit. Why would someone, a Frenchman no less, want to make a movie about the Hopi Snake Dance?"

"It's called 'The Lower World,'" Fernando replied. He went on to explain the plot of the movie, as far as Roberto had explained it to him. It sounded even crazier when he tried to explain it to someone else.

Jodie laughed. "What a crock! Thing is, Manny said the Hopi Tribal Council is sending a contingent down here to talk some sense into the move people. You can imagine what'll happen when they get here."

Fernando could indeed imagine. The rubber snakes alone would set them off big time.

"Goddamnit," Jodie continued. "Now I'll have to go down there tomorrow morning and talk to these idiots. I'm already swamped with the usual stuff, shootings and car thefts and domestic violence calls. Plus I'm short a man. One of our deputies called it quits last week."

"You want some help?" Fernando asked. "I could meet you there."

"Why don't I pick you up? That way you can fill me in on what you know about the movie. Nine o'clock okay?"

"I'll be ready," Fernando said, always willing to work with Jodie, who he admired for her hard work and dedication to the job. She was as good as it gets.

Predictably, he had a troubled sleep that night, dreaming of actors whirling around a phony movie set with rubber snakes dangling from their mouths. At one point in the dream a group of Hopi elders attacked the actors, angry at the desecration of their sacred dance by a bunch of clownish actors. When he awoke, irritated and groggy, he waited until Estelle left for work before getting out of bed and dressing. He wanted to avoid Estelle's questions this morning.

By the time Jodie arrived in her cruiser he'd had a light breakfast and was ready and waiting for her on the patio. She pulled up to the garage and honked, not seeing him on the patio. He waved and walked to the cruiser, climbing into the front passenger's seat.

"Good, you're not armed. I want to keep this civil...if at all possible," Jodie mentioned.

"I agree," Fernando said. "Enough with the fireworks."

Then Jodie noticed Fernando's forehead. "What happened to you? Walk into a door, as they say?"

Fernando laughed. "Something like that. I walked into a flying clipboard, thanks to Roberto, Durand's secretary."

"No kidding? Well, do you want to bring your gun after all...so you can shoot him?" she asked, smiling.

"Not this time, but I'll think of something," Fernando replied.

Jodie drove quickly down to the Paseo and around to Old Santa Fe

Trail. She shot out to Interstate 25 and down to the turnoff to Bonanza Creek Road.

Fernando had forgotten how fast she drove. On the way down he barely had time to tell her about Jeff Walker's death after secretly videotaping the Hopi Snake Dance at Walpi, followed by Gail Walker's murder by someone wanting the video, most likely Max Russo and the Santa Fe Film Collective, the people who'd sent Jeff Walker to Walpi, or René Durand and his secretary Roberto, all of whom were desperate to get their hands on the secret video.

"I don't get it, why do they want a video of the Hopi Snake Dance?" Jodie asked. "If they want models to follow, can't they just look online at images of the Snake Dancers?"

"Apparently Durand wants to include brief clips of the actual dance in his movie, for so-called authenticity," Fernando said. "Russo contracted with Jeff Walker, a Santa Fe photographer, to secretly tape the dance so he could sell it to Durand. Then, after Jeff's death, Durand was trying to buy the video directly from Gail Walker in order to avoid paying Russo."

Jodie glanced at Fernando. "Then money. That's the reason for all of this."

Fernando nodded. "More or less, yes."

When they entered Bonanza Creek Ranch, Fernando directed Jodie to the office. No one seemed to be around at this early hour of the morning, although several cars were parked over by the tent and picnic tables.

"Continue on down the road and bear left," Fernando said. "Durand's company is using the Mountain Cabin Set."

"Mountain cabin? Sounds almost pastoral," Jodie said sarcastically.

"There," Fernando said, pointing to the trailers parked in the same place as yesterday.

Jodie parked across the road from the movie trailers. They didn't see anyone as they climbed out of the cruiser.

"The set is up on the mesa," Fernando said.

Jodie nodded, heading up the narrow trail without saying a word. All business, as usual.

Fernando struggled to keep up with Jodie. A former athlete on the University of New Mexico's women's basketball team, she hadn't lost a step. He had no doubt she could still play a mean game of basketball.

By the time they reached the top of the mesa Fernando was out of breath. He paused to take some deep breaths, while Jodie stomped around the set getting angrier and angrier.

"What a travesty," Jodie said.

When she kicked at the canvas back-drop, Fernando thought for a moment she intended to kick or rip the canvas off its wooden frame, which might precipitate a nasty scene. Instead, she just cursed and moved on to the fake snake pit, where she picked up one of the rubber snakes and laughed. "You have to be kidding me. A goddamn rubber snake! What's wrong with these people?"

Fernando held his tongue. He didn't know where to begin.

"How's this set ever supposed to look real?" Jodie asked. "It's a joke."

"They shoot after dark with a bonfire burning over by the wall, so you probably wouldn't see much of anything except the dancers coming out of the smoke and the shadows," Fernando said. "That's my guess."

Jodie looked around a bit more and then turned to Fernando. "I've seen enough of this, let's get out of here."

Just then Fernando noticed a small car pull up beside Jodie's cruiser. A Mini Cooper, of all things. You didn't see many Mini Coopers in Santa Fe. He motioned toward the parking area at the bottom of the mesa. "Looks like we have company," he said.

Jodie, still furious, started down the trail with Fernando on her heels. Coming down the trail they saw three people climb awkwardly out of the small car: Durand, Roberto, and their driver.

"That's the director, the short guy in the sports jacket," Fernando said, pointing to Durand.

"I figured as much," Jodie said. She wasted no time. She marched up to Durand and yelled rapid fire right in his face, "What in the hell do you think you're doing here? The Hopi Snake Dance is a sacred religious ceremony not to be mimicked by idiots like you! This is not only disrespectful, it's a desecration of Hopi religion. We don't allow that in New Mexico. We take cultural appropriation seriously here, especially when it's done by a bunch of ignorant outsiders like you. It's illegal...or should be. Do you understand what I'm saying, or do I need to have one of your lackeys translate it for you?"

Fernando kept his distance, admiring Jodie's vitriol.

Roberto also kept his distance, noticing the Band Aid on Fernando's forehead. It was clear he was wary of Fernando.

The driver climbed back into the mini, a young man who looked scared to death of Jodie.

"You understand?" Jodie shouted in Durand's face, grabbing his arm and shaking him.

Durand jumped out of Jodie's grasp and waved his hands around hysterically. He spit out a string of French profanity and then asked Roberto, "*Qu'est-ce qu'elle a dit?*"

Roberto translated what Jodie had said.

"*Main non*...not a desecration, not disrespectful...*c'est de l'art, madam!*" Durand replied. "*Art! Vous comprenez?*"

"Bullshit!" Jodie yelled. "What you're doing has nothing to do with art—it's crass sensationalism...to make money!"

"*Cette femme est folle,*" Durand said, flipping his wrist up in the air. He turned and climbed back into the Mini Cooper with the driver shaking his head as he waited for Roberto to join him in the car.

"You heard the lady," Fernando hissed at Roberto, who looked uneasily at the Mini and then back to Fernando.

Time for payback.

When Roberto snarled and took a step forward, Fernando did the same, except he drove his right hand with 180 pounds of muscle as hard as he could into Roberto's gut, doubling the tall man over.

Roberto gasped and fell on his hands and knees, fortunately for him. If he hadn't fallen to his knees, Fernando would have brought his knee up into Roberto's face breaking his nose and causing a blood bath.

"You touch me again and I'll give you a beating that you will never forget," Fernando said, kicking Roberto in the side and sending him sprawling in the dirt of the parking lot.

Roberto managed to crawl to the Mini before Fernando could kick him again. He pulled himself up by the door handle and climbed inside the small car quickly before Fernando could come after him.

With that, Fernando stood back and smiled. He watched the Mini back up and then take off down to road to the office, where it parked near the tent. Probably to ask for help or to complain about their treatment.

Fernando turned to Jodie. "That went well," he quipped.

Jodie glared at Fernando. "Yeah, but I'm afraid we're gonna have quite a show when the Hopi get here."

They climbed into the cruiser and proceeded down the road. When they drove past the Mini Cooper they saw Durand, Roberto, and the driver all huddled together in the small car.

Plotting?

theory we part the Mictal Gorge or they say." Durand, Robinson, and the river
all huddled together in the small ...

Mocha

15

Jodie took her time driving back into Santa Fe. She took the Cerrillos Road exit and stopped at Café Castro for an early lunch. They discussed the available options to stop the filming of the mock snake dance. Fernando pointed out there was no law in the state preventing outsiders, even Anglos, from performing Native American Dances. Jodie said she would speak to the county district attorney about pursuing a charge of cultural appropriation under privacy law or whatever charge he could think of that would at least halt production temporarily. The hope being that Durand would tire of waiting around and lose interest.

"I might have better luck with the county district attorney, because the county isn't nearly as head-over-heels in love with the movie industry as the city seems to be," Jodie said. "Anything for a buck. The city is not much different than the movie people, really."

Fernando nodded. "That's true, but I don't know about the county district attorney. I already talked to Steve Chabot about a court order to stop production. He seemed dubious, said he wouldn't request a court order because the law is too murky. Difficult to prosecute cultural appropriation or copyright violation, whatever you decide to call it."

Jodie didn't give up easily. "Well, I'll talk to Steve too if I have to. Maybe we can think of something else to charge them with. How about inciting a riot when the Hopis get here and start raising hell?"

Fernando laughed. "Worth a try. You might even call the Hopi Tribal Office. Manny may have called them, but I don't know what exactly he told them. Maybe they would try to get a court order."

"I will," Jodie said. "The Tribal Office is at Kykotsmovi Village. I don't know who the Governor is these days. Used to be Tim N. I never could pronounce his name, so I always called him Governor N."

By the time Jodie dropped him off at home the sun had long since passed its zenith. He went directly into his study and booted up his laptop, hoping to study up on Hopi Tribal Law. He'd barely sat down when a text message pinged on his phone nearby. He clicked on the text and read: "24 hours." The sender was none other than Cody Hunt of City Different Security.

Fernando put away his laptop and went out to the patio to think. He needed a plan. What would he do if Cody showed up in his driveway again tomorrow? He couldn't expect help from Manny or Jodie, since both were busy with their official duties. So he decided to call on Blaine Rogers, who he'd used several times for backup. Blaine might be a drunk and a loudmouth, but he was also intimidating and strong as an ox. Plus he knew how to use the Glock he kept in his office desk, thanks to a stint in the military that ended when Blaine decked his sergeant for barking out one too many orders and was dishonorably discharged.

Cody did his best pretending to be a tough guy, but he would be no match for crazy Blaine.

No time like the present, he decided. He locked the house and climbed into his Cherokee, driving down to the Paseo and around to Canyon Road. Blaine and Tessa's gallery, Picasso and Co., was a couple of blocks past Delgado Street. They'd been fighting about the name since Tessa joined Blaine and merged her Abiquiu gallery with his. Tessa hated the name Picasso and Co., but Blaine hated all the alternatives Tessa proposed. The result was stalemate.

Fernando parked in the lot beside Picasso and Co. and walked up to the porch. When he opened the heavy wooden door he heard Blaine's booming voice in the front gallery. He peeked around the corner and saw Blaine, dressed in his typical red Bermuda shorts and white T-shirt, speaking to an elderly couple, both of whom were dressed in Western garb. The husband wore a white ten-gallon hat and the wife had ratted red hair that puffed up to the height of her husband's ten-gallon hat. Tourists. Probably from Texas.

"These famous abstracts were done by the late Santa Fe painter Jimmy Mackey, who died tragically a couple of years ago, murdered in Taos by a bunch of hooligans," Blaine said, pointing to a collection of Jimmy's

'Chopped Nudes,' as Jimmy called the paintings. Nudes of women with multiple limbs growing out of various parts of their bodies.

The red-haired woman put on her reading glasses to take a closer look. "My gawd, Morris, they's a leg growing outta that woman's ear and an arm growing out of her cooter."

Now the husband was interested. He moved closer to take a look, nodding his appreciation.

Blaine laughed and said "Yes, madam, that's in the tradition of the great Picasso himself—the fragmented self, and so forth...."

Fernando stepped into the office to wait until Blaine finished with his customers. He found Tessa sitting at the big mahogany desk in the center of the office pouring over computer print-outs.

"Hi, Tessa," what's up?

"I'm trying to keep up the books," Tessa responded. "Blaine doesn't know shit about bookkeeping. You should have seen the mess they were in when I arrived. He owes me big time."

Fernando laughed. "I can believe that—hell, he's rarely sober."

"Yeah, I'm trying to get him to cut down on his drinking. You know, more moderate like me."

"Gimme a break, you're not a moderate drinker," Blaine bellowed as he suddenly walked into the office. "You drink every bit as much as your big sister Ruby, maybe more."

"No way!" Tessa shot back. "She's a drunk."

Fernando held up his hands. "You guys want me to come back later after you've settle your who's-a-drunk debate?"

Both Blaine and Tessa gave him the Evil Eye.

"Blaine, I came to ask for your help," Fernando said, changing the topic. "I could use back up again."

"Hah! Who's after you now?" Blaine asked. "For someone who's retired, you sure attract a lot of trouble?"

Fernando sighed. "That I do, sorry to say. Long story. It starts with Jeff Walker, the photographer. I think you know him. He was paid by the Santa Fe Film Collective to secretly videotape the Hopi Snake Dance. He died in an apparent accident on his way back to Santa Fe, but the video ended up in the hands of his wife Gail, who was murdered by someone trying to get possession of the tape—either the film collective or the movie production that intended to buy the video from the collective.

These people know, or at least suspect, that I have a copy of the video. One of the security guards working for the collective gave me forty-eight hours to give them the video. A guy by the name of Cody Hunt. The forty-eight hours are up tomorrow morning."

"Wait a minute," Blaine said. "Fess up. Do you, or do you not, have a copy of the video?"

Fernando nodded. "I do. I made a copy. It's on my iphone."

"Then why don't you just send them a copy and tell 'em to fuck off?" Tessa asked.

Damn good question. Why didn't he? He didn't exactly know himself. It had something to do with not wanting to participate in this desecration of Hopi culture, but it was personal too. He didn't like to be pushed around or threatened, not by Russo or Roberto or anyone.

"I don't know," Fernando said after a long pause. "It just doesn't seem right to let them use a video of a sacred Hopi dance in their ridiculous goddamn movie. Two people have died already. How many more? Everything about this leaves a bad taste in my mouth. I'm sorry I ever got involved."

"No shit, you should be," Blaine said. "I hope you know there's a longstanding curse on all outsiders who try to steal the Hopi Snake Dance."

"So I'm told," Fernando said.

"Okay, as long as you know. So what do you want me to do?" Blaine asked finally.

"I think this Cody Hunt will show up at my house tomorrow morning," Fernando said. "He may not be alone. Can you come over about eight a.m.? That way we'll be waiting for them."

"Sure—it's not like I have anything better to do like run a gallery!" Blaine said, sarcastically.

"I owe you big time," Fernando said.

"Yes you do. I'll add it to your tab."

16

From the moment he awoke Fernando worried that Blaine or Cody Hunt would arrive before Estelle left for work. Whatever happened, he wanted to keep Estelle out of it. This was his problem. He had to deal with it.

When Estelle got up at her usual 6:30, Fernando quickly slipped on his clothes and went into the bathroom. He noticed the goddamn Band Aid had fallen off his forehead, lost somewhere among the bed covers. Didn't look so bad this morning, just a little red, so he said the hell with it and did his business without replacing the Band Aid on his forehead.

When finished, he headed for the kitchen. He brewed a pot of coffee and made a cheese and green chile omelet while Estelle showered. This was a novelty for Fernando, who generally had a hard time waking up. He usually required a couple cups of coffee before attempting to do anything in the morning, especially cooking. He rarely made breakfast.

When Estelle appeared in the kitchen, dressed for work, she stopped in the doorway, mouth open. "What's this? I haven't seen you make breakfast for the two of us in months. What's the occasion?"

"No occasion. I just felt like making you breakfast this morning," Fernando replied.

Estelle looked at him suspiciously. "Uh-huh."

Nervous, Fernando remained on edge during breakfast, expecting to hear a vehicle turn into their driveway at any given moment. Estelle noticed his nervousness but held her tongue. They finished a few minutes before eight, which was when Estelle usually left for work. By the time she'd made her lunch and gathered together what she needed for work it was a quarter past eight.

Fernando breathed a sigh of relief when Estelle said goodbye and walked out to her Camry. When he heard the Camry pull out of their driveway onto Acequia Madre, he went into his study and strapped on the holster holding his Smith & Wesson. As ready as he would ever be, he went outside to the patio and sat on his bench with a cup of coffee, waiting for Blaine to arrive. The big man was already late, which wasn't surprising given Blaine's drinking and erratic behavior. Sometimes you could count on him, sometimes not.

That didn't change matters. Fact is, he needed Blaine. With the one exception of Antonio, who'd moved to Colorado to help his son operate a ranch, no one could intimidate like Blaine could intimidate. The man was irreplaceable.

He waited another ten and then fifteen minutes, still no Blaine. Now he began to worry in earnest. He might have to face Cody alone. So how did he want to do this? He decided to pull the Cherokee up to the narrowest part of the driveway to block Cody from getting anywhere near his house. That was a start.

Cursing Blaine, he walked over to his Cherokee and drove up the driveway, wedging the big vehicle sideways in the drive. It was the best he could do. Let the show begin.

He climbed out of the Cherokee and leaned back against its front fender waiting. He rested his right hand on the holster, inches from his Smith & Wesson. He had an extra clip in his pocket, if needed.

Minutes later Fernando heard and then saw the City Different Security truck coming down Acequia Madre. Fuck! His body tensed at the thought of having to deal with Cody all by his lonesome.

The panel truck turned into his driveway and stopped about ten yards from the Cherokee. Seeming surprised, Cody sat in the driver's seat staring at Fernando leaning against the Cherokee. He made no effort to get out of the panel truck for several long seconds. Finally he opened the door and stepped into the driveway, still staring at Fernando.

Then Fernando saw another man sitting in the passenger's seat of the panel truck. Looked like Wes Snyder, trying to hunker down to make himself invisible as if he wanted nothing to do with this business.

"We want the video," Cody said.

"I told you, I don't have the video," Fernando said.

"No, but you have a copy," Cody replied, angry now. "We know you have a copy."

With that, Cody took a step forward into Fernando's face. He poked Fernando in the chest. "Give us the video...or we'll go in your house and find it ourselves, even if we have to tear up your house."

Incensed, Fernando pushed Cody back and said, "Yeah, I have the fucking video, but you'll never get your hands on it!"

In response Cody launched a left hook. Fernando ducked, but the punch grazed him on the chin and sent him reeling to the side. Fernando managed to grab hold of the Cherokee to keep from falling.

Just then Blaine's Ford Bronco turned into the driveway. The white Bronco skidded to a stop behind the panel truck. Blaine jumped out wearing his red Bermuda shorts and white T-shirt and ran around the panel truck like a crazily dressed NFL linebacker chasing a quarterback.

"What the fuck!" Blaine yelled, seeing Cody standing over Fernando, still hanging on to the Cherokee.

The big man grabbed the surprised Cody by the shirt collar and spun him around, ripping his shirt nearly off. He slammed Cody back into the panel truck so hard that Cody's head bounced off the truck like a basketball. Then, raging now, Blaine grabbed Cody by the neck and slammed his head back into the truck even harder than before, sending the smaller Cody slithering to the ground, where he sat and stared blankly up at Blaine.

Blaine pivoted around and saw Wes trying to hide in the passenger's seat of the panel truck. He opened the door and grabbed Wes around the neck with his left hand, choking him.

Wes squirmed out of Blaine's grasp and yelled, "I have nothing to do with this. He made me come along. I'm not involved. Leave me alone!"

"Then stay away from here," Blaine snarled.

Wes nodded, cowering on the seat.

Blaine slammed the door closed and came back to Cody, still dazed and sitting on his ass. He kicked Cody in the side to rouse him and then grabbed his torn shirt and pulled him to his feet. "You come here again or lay a finger on Fernando again, I'll break both of your arms. You understand?"

Cody nodded weakly.

Blaine shoved him toward the driver's door of the panel truck.

Cody fell on his hands and knees and struggled to stand up, holding on to the door of the panel truck. He finally made it into the truck, scooting over behind the steering wheel.

Fernando watched the panel truck back up and then, stopping and starting, turn onto Acequia Madre where it swerved out in front of a speeding BMW. The driver of the BMW slammed on his brakes and honked. The two vehicles proceeded toward the Paseo with the panel truck stopping and starting and the BMW honking all the way down to the Paseo.

"Thanks," Fernando said to Blaine.

"No problem, sorry I was late," Blaine said. "Tessa always wants morning sex. She wakes up horny–all wet and juicy."

Fernando raised his hands. "No more details, please."

Blaine laughed. "Tell that to Tessa."

"You didn't even bring your Glock," Fernando said, noticing Blaine wasn't packing.

"Nah—I don't need a gun with these bozos," Blaine replied. "They're amateurs...all hat and no substance."

17

After Blaine drove off, Fernando climbed into his Cherokee and drove back down to the garage. He always parked in front, to leave their one-car garage for Estelle's Camry, if she wanted it. Usually she parked in the drive next to his Cherokee, but on the odd occasion she liked to park in the garage. He felt a bit rattled after the encounter and somewhat surprised by the intensity of Blaine's rage. He knew the big man could be a beast, but this time he'd worried Blaine would actually kill Cody with his bare hands. That would have created a messy situation, to say the least.

The upside was that Cody would almost certainly not bother him again, not after the beating he'd taken today and Blaine's warning to stay away. He had but one regret. He probably shouldn't have admitted that he had a copy of the Snake Dance video. That might come back to bite him.

Curious, he wondered why Max Russo and René Durand were so desperate to get their hands on the video. Admittedly he'd watched the video quickly, not paying much attention to the technical quality of the film, but he remembered it suffered from poor lighting and an excruciatingly slow pace. Much too slow for today's movies, gone to fast-paced thrillers and apocalyptic roller-coasters.

With that in mind, Fernando went into his study and sat at the desk with his cell phone. He clicked on the video and watched it more carefully this time. Same reaction. The lighting was impossibly dark and murky, thanks to the smoke and the absence of adequate lighting. Moreover, the first half of the video—the preliminary dancing and singing—went on far too long, as boring as he remembered it. Only when the snake dancers appeared did the film pick up, with striking visuals and a brisk pace as the dancers pranced around the dusty plaza with the writhing snakes dangling from their mouths. Short clips from this part of the movie might be of interest. At most a couple of minutes.

Sitting back in his desk chair for a moment, he decided to revisit his copy of D. H. Lawrence's *Mornings in Mexico* and look again at Lawrence's memoir of attending a Hopi Snake Dance. He took the book out of his top drawer, where he'd put it after rescuing the book from a paper bag meant for the trash. This time he read more slowly, examining Lawrence's loose prose and even looser descriptions of the Hopi. As before, he found the English novelist's prose overblown and cluttered with wild generalizations about the Hopi and Native Americans in general, which Lawrence knew next to noting about. He read:

"They say that the twelve officiating men of the snake clan of the tribe have for nine days ben hunting snakes in the rocks. They have been performing the mysteries for nine days, in the kiva, and for two days they have fasted completely. All these days they have tended the snakes, washed them, and exchanged spirits with them. The spirit of man soothing and seeking and making interchange with the spirits of the snakes. For the snakes are more rudimentary, nearer to the great convulsive powers. Nearer to the nameless Sun, more knowing in the slanting tracks of the rain, the pattering of the invisible feet of the rain-monster from the sky. The snakes are man's next emissaries to the rain-gods. The snakes lie nearer to the source of potency, the dark, lurking, intense sun at the center of the earth."

After a few pages of this nonsense, Lawrence mercifully turns his attention to the Snake Dance and the memoir improves a bit. Still filled with hyperbole and wild generalizations, though. So much so that Fernando had to stop reading. Instead, he tossed the book in his wastebasket.

Moments later his cell phone rang. He didn't recognize the number as he picked up the phone but clicked accept anyway.

"Mister Lopez," a vaguely familiar voice said. "Max Russo here. Listen, I'm sorry about this morning. Cody misunderstood my instructions. I wonder if we could talk quietly somewhere, just the two of us, over coffee? Would you be available to meet at the Starbuck's just off the Plaza this afternoon? Say two o'clock?"

Meeting Russo was the last thing Fernando wanted to do. On the other hand, it could provide a way to finally put an end to this ordeal. What did he have to lose by meeting for coffee?

"Okay, I suppose, as long as you come alone," Fernando said. "None of your goons."

Russo laughed. "None of my goons."

Fernando clicked off. He ate a light lunch and called Manny to find out if he had any news about the Gail Walker murder investigation. Manny told him that Cody had stopped in for fingerprinting yesterday and that he was clean. That is, Forensics had not found his fingerprints in Gail Walker's house.

A few minutes before two o'clock Fernando drove down Acequia Madre to the Paseo and around to Alameda Street. He parked along the river, where he always parked, and walked up Old Santa Fe Trail to the Plaza, swarming with tourists this afternoon. He made his way through the crowd on San Francisco Street down to the Starbuck's at the end of the block.

Inside, he didn't see Russo at first because of the line of customers waiting to order. Then he spotted him sitting at a rear table holding a tall coffee in a paper cup and looking his button-down best. Russo waved.

Fernando nodded as the line inched forward. After he ordered and picked up his coffee, he joined Russo at the rear table.

"Shall we go out on the Plaza...get some fresh air while we talk?" Russo asked. "What do you think?"

'Why not," Fernando said, following Russo outside and across the street to the Plaza. They sat on a bench overlooking the plywood box the weak-kneed Mayor in all his wisdom had placed over what remained of the obelisk celebrating Union soldiers that had fought in the Civil War. The obelisk had been pulled down by angry demonstrators a few years back and never replaced because no one could seem to agree on what to replace it with. All too familiar in Santa Fe, a city of three distinct cultures that had lived uncomfortably with each other for over four hundred years.

Russo smiled. "Nice day." He'd adopted an entirely different persona than the last time Fernando had seen him. Instead of acerbic and prickly, he was doing his best to project a friendly, outgoing personality. A real salesman. It wasn't difficult to guess what Russo was selling.

"Again, I'm sorry about what happened this morning," Russo said. "I don't know what got into Cody, that's not how we do business."

Fernando nodded, letting Russo talk. He didn't believe a word Russo said and had nothing to say to him in response.

Russo pointed to the red wound on Fernando's forehead. "I hope Toby didn't do that."

"No, someone else had that honor," Fernando replied. "No need to worry about me. You should worry about Toby. If he comes near me again, my backup man Blaine just might kill him. He almost did that today."

"So I heard," Russo said. "The whole incident was unfortunate. Should never have happened."

Fernando shrugged. What did Russo want him to say?

"Well...so I wondered if you would reconsider giving us a copy of the Snake Dance video," Russo continued, moving into his sales pitch. "We're a big part of the movie industry here. We provide logistics and find movie sets and equity actors for the film companies shooting here. As you know, the movie industry is vital to the economy of Santa Fe and all of New Mexico, the entire state. Before long, revenues from the movie industry will replace big oil...and we're a lot cleaner," he said, chuckling, playing at being friendly.

Fernando cleared his throat. He spoke slowly, wanting to be understood. "As I see it, the problem with using the video in your movies is two-fold. First, it was illegally obtained, stolen. That to me constitutes cultural appropriation, whether or not the district attorney is willing to file charges. Second, using it for profit would be disrespectful and a desecration of Hopi religion.

Russo frowned, beginning to lose his nice guy act.

"Not to mention the murder of Gail Walker...to get your hands on the video," Fernando added.

Russo raised his free hand. "Wait. We had nothing to do with Gail Walker's murder. Cody went in for fingerprinting yesterday. You can ask the detective about that. I forget his name."

"Manny Alvarez?"

"Yes, that's him," Russo said. "We had nothing to do with Gail Walker's murder. In fact, we were working with her, trying to buy the video. Murdering her would be the last thing we would do."

Fernando took a long drink of coffee, considering what Russo had just said. It made sense, sort of.

"The thing is, we would only use short clips of the video, just to give authenticity to the films that might want to use it."

"Like 'The Lower World,'" Fernando added.

Russo glared at Fernando. "Yes, but how do you know about 'The Lower World?'"

"Because the director, René Durand, tried to buy the video from me," Fernando replied.

"René Durand tried to buy it from you? That sonofabitch! He's double-crossing me," Russo said, mostly to himself. He glanced around the Plaza, as if looking for something or someone.

Fernando saw an opening and took it. "Yeah...made me a good offer, as a matter of fact."

Furious, Russo stood up and poured his coffee on the grass and then, without a word to Fernando, stomped off toward San Francisco Street.

Fernando watched Russo disappear in the crowd of tourists. Smiling, he leaned back on the bench and sipped his coffee.

Let Russo and Durand devour each other and leave him alone.

18

Sitting in the Plaza always relaxed Fernando. He'd done some of his best thinking here, trying to make decisions about personal matters or professional moves. Back when he was lead detective at the Santa Fe Police Department, he came here often to brood about difficult cases. Today, though, he just wanted to relax, tired of dealing with Cody and Max Russo and the rest of those involved in this Hopi Snake Dance video business. He closed his eyes and let the sun, already sinking in the western sky, bask him in sunshine.

He wasn't aware of how long he'd sat there daydreaming until a woman's voice brought him to the here and now. "Do you mind if I join you?" she asked, carrying a Starbuck's cup and paper bag.

"No, please, have a seat," he said. "I was just leaving."

With that, Fernando got up and walked to the nearby trash bin and tossed in his empty paper cup. He walked back down Old Santa Fe Trail to the river and climbed into his Cherokee.

Everybody wanted the damn video, including Gail, who died trying to sell it for a few extra bucks. He thought again about just giving both Russo and Durand copies and being done with it. Problem was, he didn't like to be bullied or told what to do. Never had. Especially by outsiders who showed up in Santa Fe making demands without knowing anything about the three cultures that made Santa Fe so unique. Insult one of the three, you insult all three. That's what he thought anyway.

Brooding, Fernando took his time driving home. His talks with Manny and Steve Chabot about legal action against Russo and Durand had frustrated him. He thought both Manny and Chabot were being too fussy, too fine in their legal opinions. Forget about cultural appropriation and intellectual property copyright, it seemed to Fernando that the real violation related to simple privacy law. It was illegal to enter someone's private property and film, especially if the property was clearly marked with no trespassing signs. The Hopi Snake Dance was held on private property where the Hopis had a "reasonable expectation of privacy." Outsiders were not allowed at the dance as clearly stated online and in signs on the Hopi's three mesas. So why the hesitation to secure a court order to stop production of a movie that intended to use a secret video illegally filmed at Hopi?

If only Raoul Garcia were still alive. The best criminal lawyer in the state of New Mexico, Raoul would take on anyone, anytime. Raoul would jump at the opportunity to stop a bunch of Anglo outsiders from desecrating Native American culture in his beloved New Mexico. What a loss.

Feeling righteous, and wishing he'd gone to law school, Fernando walked into his house and booted up his laptop. He spent the remainder of the afternoon on his computer, looking for case law involving individuals who violated Native American rituals or religious ceremonies. Sadly, each case proved unique, involving a specific set of circumstances, so by the time Estelle came home from work Fernando was more confused than ever. Maybe it wasn't as simple as he hoped or as privacy law seem to promise.

Over dinner Fernando told Estelle more about the standoff—if you wanted to call it that—at Bonanza Creek Ranch. She listened to his theory of privacy law and how the surreptitiously taped video would be a violation of privacy law, but Estelle just shook her head. "I don't think you'll ever get a prosecutor here to go after anyone or anything in the film industry because the industry has become the lifeblood of Santa Fe. Money talks, my friend. It's as simple as that."

After listening to Estelle, Fernando had pretty much come to accept her point of view. Not surprising, because Estelle always cut to the chase. She didn't dilly-dally around the edges or the what-ifs of a question. She went right to the heart of the matter, which in this case was money.

He went to bed exhausted, tired of thinking about the movie. He just wanted to sleep and wake up tomorrow refreshed and ready for something new, anything but the goddamn movie.

Unfortunately, his sleep lasted all of two hours. The ringing of his cell phone woke him at half past eleven.

"What the...I thought I told you to leave your phone in the study!" Estelle said, angrily.

Fernando fumbled for his phone. When he saw Manny's name on the screen, he grabbed it and stumbled into the hallway. He made it to his study and collapsed in his desk chair.

"Sorry to bother you so late," Manny said when Fernando clicked on. "We've had some trouble tonight—I thought you might want to know because it involves this Snake Dance video, we think."

Fernando was too tired to speak.

"Someone reported a shooting in the La Fonda garage about eleven o'clock," Manny continued. "When we got there, we found Roberto Alvarado dead. He works with the movie director, René Durand."

"I know who he is," Fernando said, finally.

"Forensics is on the way, if you want to join us for some late night fun," Manny said.

"Yeah, right," Fernando replied and then changed his mind. "Okay, I'm on my way."

Fernando crept back in the bedroom and grabbed his clothes. Estelle was either sleeping or had decided to ignore him. Once dressed, he left the house, making sure to lock the kitchen door behind him, and climbed into his Cherokee. He drove downtown and parked on Cathedral Place, near La Fonda. He saw the bright lights in the La Fonda Parking Garage as he came around the corner of San Francisco Street. Police cars lined the street.

Inside the garage he saw Manny standing in the rear of the garage talking to Miguel from Forensics. Several other officers walked around the garage searching for evidence.

Fernando saw the body as he approached. Roberto lay flat on his back on the concrete floor of the garage. Two blood-soaked holes stained the center of Roberto's long-sleeve polo shirt. His mouth remained open, frozen in a look of surprise at whoever shot him.

"He had this note in his hand," Manny said, handing Fernando a hand-written note on a small piece of paper. The note read: "I have something you want. Meet me in the rear of the La Fonda Parking Garage at eleven."

Fernando studied the note. The something Roberto wanted must have been the video. And whoever pulled the trigger must have known that Roberto desperately wanted the video.

"Must be the Snake Dance video," Fernando said.

Manny nodded, deep in thought. Finally he said, "An eye for an eye."

Confused, Fernando asked, "What do you mean?"

"We fingerprinted him earlier today," Manny said. "His fingerprints were all over Gail Walker's house."

"No kidding," Fernando said. "So he killed Gail Walker...and now someone killed him."

That made three victims of the curse so far, the curse for stealing the Hopi Snake Dance.

"Looks like it. Wait...what happened to you?" Manny asked, noticing the red wound on Fernando's forehead.

Fernando pointed to Roberto. "He hit me with a clipboard last night when I went out to spy on the movie set."

"Tit for tat," Manny mumbled.

While they talked Miguel came over, wearing gloves and a mask. "I'm nearly done here. The time of death was shortly after eleven. The cause is obvious. I might know more tomorrow. I'll come back first thing and look around in the daylight. We'll see."

Fernando kept Manny company for another hour, until Roberto's body had been taken away and the yellow caution tape had been installed to block off the crime scene area.

"Fuck...it's almost two o'clock," Manny said. "You want to get some early breakfast?"

Fernando laughed. "I gotta get some sleep."

"Tell me about it," Manny said.

Fernando waved as he made his way out of the garage into the dark night. Driving home he kept thinking about Roberto, who he'd misjudged big time. At first Roberto seemed so docile, like Durand's boy toy. Obviously not.

What else had he misjudged?

19

Fernando's eyes seemed glued shut. He finally managed to open them one at a time with great effort. Then he fumbled for the clock on the nightstand. Past ten o'clock. He couldn't remember ever sleeping this late. He'd always been a morning person, eager to get up for his morning coffee. This morning he felt like a corpse, exhausted and unable to move his tired, aching body. No surprise, since he hadn't made it home last night until nearly three o'clock.

He fought his way out from under the blankets and hobbled into the bathroom, where he examined the wound on his forehead, which had begun to itch. The stitches looked redder this morning, so he opened a bottle of alcohol and dabbed at the wound. Didn't look infected. He figured the redness must be from tossing and turning on the pillow and decided to ignore it.

Looking around the bedroom for his clothes, Fernando remembered he'd undressed in the living room last night, so as not to wake Estelle. He found his clothes thrown on the sofa, his hiking boots kicked off over by the window. He slipped into his jeans and boots and then tossed his dirty shirt in the laundry room on his way to the kitchen.

Estelle hadn't left him any coffee this morning, so he brewed himself a cup in his Keurig and took it outside to the patio. Wearing only a T-shirt, he felt a chill in the air this morning, mostly because of a breeze blowing in from the northwest. That time of year. Wouldn't be long before the cold weather would descend on Santa Fe. As he'd aged he'd come to hate the winter months. At seven thousand feet above sea level, Santa Fe could get damn cold in the winter with too much snow. Land of the dead, that's what winter was to him.

After a second cup of coffee Fernando's head began to clear. Whenever he closed his eyes, he saw Roberto lying on the concrete floor of the La Fonda Parking Garage with two bullet holes in his chest. He would no longer have to worry about Roberto— someone else had already taken care of that. But he would need to visit Ruby and tell her the news, since she'd asked him to find Gail's killer. That's how he got involved in all this. Thanks to Ruby.

The question now became who killed Roberto. All the evidence pointed to one of the yahoos at the Santa Fe Film Collective. Cody, a common thug, would be the obvious choice, maybe too obvious. Fernando couldn't completely rule out Max Russo, who'd lost his cool in the Plaza upon learning that Roberto was trying to go around the collective and make a deal to buy the video directly from Gail. And what about Wes Snyder, the drugstore cowboy? Snyder was difficult to read. Fernando did not have a take on him just yet.

One way to find out. Fernando decided he would pay the Film Collective yahoos a visit. He went back into the house and finished dressing, buckling on his holster. Then he drove around to Old Pecos Trail and up to the Santa Fe Armory for the Arts. He parked the Cherokee and slammed the door, putting on his tough guy face. He didn't have anything to fear from these guys, Fernando told himself. By now all of them knew he could call in the reserves if needed—and none of them wanted to mess with big bad Blaine.

He entered the Armory and walked down the long hallway in his best swagger. When he opened the door to the Film Collective, he found Wes Snyder standing in the door to the inner office talking to Max Russo.

Snyder turned to look at Fernando. "What do you want?" he asked, not in a friendly way. Big surprise.

"Who is it?" Russo asked from the inner office.

"Lopez," Snyder responded. "You want me to throw him out?"

Fernando smiled. "That's the second time you've asked to throw me out—I didn't know I was that popular," he said, brushing Snyder aside with his right arm and walking past him into the inner office.

Russo sat at his desk, across from a red-faced Cody hunkered down in an armchair facing the desk. Cody's face was swollen from the beat-down Blaine had given him.

"To what do we owe this honor?" Russo asked, a pained expression on his face. "Did you change your mind about the video?"

"I wanna know which one of you killed Roberto Alvarado?" Fernando said, point blank. No words wasted.

Both Russo and Cody stared at the holster on Fernando's hip. Neither spoke. The silence was deafening.

Finally Russo cleared his throat and then said, "Well...I'll give you credit...you have a lotta balls coming in here and asking that."

"Which one of you?" Fernando repeated, his hand on his Smith & Wesson.

Russo raised his hand. "Sorry to disappoint you, but none of us killed Roberto. Why would we want to kill him? We were trying to sell him the video."

"You don't have the video—I do," Fernando said, seeing a flash of anger in Russo's face now.

Cody coughed in his chair. "How about this, you give us the video and I'll tell you who killed Roberto," he said.

"Cody!" Russo snapped, obviously not happy with the direction of the conversation.

"Tell you the truth, I really don't give a damn about the video any more," Fernando said. "Three people have died so far. That's what I care about. How many more?"

Russo shrugged.

Fernando walked over to Cody and put his hand on the back of the armchair. "Okay, you have a deal. You tell me who killed Roberto and I'll give you the video. I'll be waiting."

With that, Fernando turned and walked to the door. Snyder backed away, making room for him to exit. "And you—stay out of my way," he warned Snyder and left the office without looking back.

20

Fernando didn't have to wait long. Wes Snyder called that afternoon, the first of the three Santa Fe Film Collective yahoos wanting to make a deal. "Okay, I'm ready," Snyder said simply, not bothering to explain further. "Why don't we meet in Cathedral Park on the north side of the cathedral? I'll be sitting on one of the benches. Say three o'clock?"

"I'll be there," Fernando said, not worried about meeting him in such a public place.

That gave him time to make a plan. Would he really hand over the video? Earlier he'd just wanted to get rid of the damn thing. Now he wondered if that was such a good idea. Why participate in the desecration? And why bring down the curse of the Hopi Snake Dance on himself, if the curse was real? He neither believed nor disbelieved in curses, ghosts, etc. But why take a chance?

Maybe he could somehow finesse the situation. Give Snyder a doctored version of the video, something like that. If he altered the video, maybe he wouldn't have to worry about the curse.

But how could he doctor the video? If he tried to change the technical qualities—the lighting, the focus, etc.—Snyder or someone else at Santa Fe Film Collective could just change them back. Instead, he decided to try something much bolder. He would make a copy of the video and then delete everything after the Snake Dancers appeared. The copy he would give Snyder then would have the drumming and chanting but not the dancing. At least not the Snake Dance with the performers holding snakes in their mouths.

Following his plan, he made a second copy of the video and then fast forwarded the copy until just before the Snake Dancers appeared. Then he deleted the rest of the video. He was ready.

When the time came Fernando drove down to Cathedral Place and parked at one of the meters. He walked around to the front of Saint Francis Cathedral and into the adjoining park, heading north toward the bronze statue commemorating the Spanish settlers of Santa Fe (as if Santa Fe hadn't been 'settled' before the Europeans arrived!). Sitting at one of the metal benches near the statue was Wes Snyder, all spiffed up in a yellow western shirt with pearl buttons and fringe along its sleeve. Looked like a department store manikin, a real dandy. The only thing missing from his outfit was a ten-gallon hat.

"Did you bring it?" Snyder asked.

"Sure, it's on my iphone," Fernando said, taking a seat on the bench next to Snyder.

Snyder nodded, eyeing Fernando suspiciously. It was clear that he didn't trust Fernando.

"Okay, tell me who killed Roberto and I'll email you a copy of the video," Fernando said.

Snyder didn't like that. "Wait a minute, you were the one who suggested this swap—it's on you to go first."

"Okay—give me your email address," Fernando said. He typed the address Snyder gave him into a new message and then uploaded the abbreviated copy of the Snake Dance video. He clicked send and herd the ping on Snyder's phone. "Done," he said, turning to Snyder.

Snyder downloaded the video on his phone and clicked the play button. After watching for a couple of minutes, he seemed satisfied and put the phone back in his shirt pocket.

"So who killed Roberto?" Fernando asked.

"Cody killed him, of course?" Snyder replied. "He's the muscle in the Collective, as you've seen. He takes care of security and all the physical problems involved. He's a real brute."

Fernando nodded. This was what he expected to hear. Cody seemed the most likely candidate—and the most capable of carrying out the shooting. And yet something about Snyder struck him as suspicious. Snyder seemed a little too eager to cast blame on Cody.

"So is Russo still planning to go ahead with selling this video to René Durand?" Fernando asked.

"Yeah, why wouldn't he? It's what he does—provide material and equipment to the movie productions that come through Santa Fe."

"Well, because three people have already died," Fernando said. "Maybe it's time to find another, safer way to make a few bucks. That's his priority, right? Profit?"

Snyder shrugged. He stood to go, patted his cell phone and said, "Thanks. Been a pleasure dealing with you."

Fernando smiled, imagining Snyder's reaction when he had a chance to view the entire video. He'd change his tune big time. Fortunately, Snyder didn't appear to be much of a threat.

He watched Snyder walk out of the park and then followed, going down East Palace to the Shed Restaurant, where he picked up a couple jars of their famous red chile. In his humble opinion the Shed had the best red chile in Santa Fe. He liked to keep a good supply on hand. Then he walked back to his Cherokee and considered his options. It was too early for Happy Hour at El Farol, so he drove up to the Paseo and headed home.

When he turned into his driveway, he almost collided with the now notorious panel truck. What now?

A smiling Max Russo walked around the front of the brown truck and held up his hand. "We come in peace," he shouted.

Fernando parked on the opposite side of the driveway and climbed out of his Cherokee. He saw Cody hunkered down behind the steering wheel in the van, a look of pure hate on his face.

"We accept your deal," Russo said. "You give us the video and we'll tell you who killed Roberto."

Confused, it took Fernando a moment to figure out they knew nothing about his meeting with Wes Snyder. That struck him as odd. Wes must be trying to double cross Russo, his boss. Maybe all of them were trying to double cross each other, who knew? He decided to say nothing about Snyder just to hear what they had to say.

"Are you still ready to deal?" Russo asked.

"Sure," Fernando said. "First you tell me who killed Roberto."

Russo laughed and shook his head. "No way, I can't be sure you would actually send me the video."

"Okay, give me your email address and I'll send the video first," Fernando said, taking out his cell phone.

After Russo provided his email address, Fernando once again

uploaded the abbreviated version of the Snake Dance and clicked send. Russo's phone dinged, which made Russo smile.

"Okay, now tell me who killed Roberto," Fernando said.

"No problem...Wes killed Roberto," Russo replied.

At first Fernando thought he'd misheard Russo. "Wes?"

"Yes, you might find it hard to believe, but Wes can be downright vicious," Russo said. "He and Roberto have had words before. And Roberto always made it worse. He was always making fun of Wes' sexual preference, as they say. You did know Wes is gay, right?"

Fernando shrugged. "Not really."

"Anyway, it's good to do business with you—finally!" Russo said, climbing back into the panel truck, eager to be off.

Fernando watched them drive off on Acequia Madre Street. He didn't know what to think. Who killed Roberto? Was it Cody or Wes? Cody seemed more likely, but it was hard to discount Russo's account. Russo had one thing that Wes didn't have—the semblance of credibility, for whatever that was worth. A semblance was just that—a semblance.

He drove the Cherokee down the driveway and parked next to their garage. He sat in the Cherokee for a few minutes brooding. What would Russo and the others do when they realized the video he'd given them was doctored, with the snake dancing cut out completely? Maybe he would know for sure who killed Roberto by their response to the bastardized video.

Now that he was home, Fernando decided to call it a day. Time to take it easy, try to forget about the video and all the trouble it had caused everyone. Once inside, he went directly to their refrigerator and grabbed a Modelo. He took the Modelo and his cell phone outside to his patio and collapsed on his favorite bench. His troubles seemed to melt away the more beer he drank. Or so he thought.

Just as he finished his Modelo and rose to get another, a message pinged on his cell phone. He thought it might be Estelle texting to tell him she would be late for dinner tonight.

Then he glanced at the screen and saw the name: Max Russo, the last person he wanted to hear from tonight.

"Nice Try," Russo texted. "We had a deal...and sadly you did not live up to your part. This means we will have to resort to other means."

Other means?

21

Fernando awoke from a deep sleep to someone whispering in his ear and shaking him by the shoulder. "Fernando, wake up, I hear someone in the house," Estelle was saying.

"What?" Fernando muttered, half asleep.

"Wake up! Didn't you hear that noise? Someone's in the house," Estelle said, shaking him harder now. "Sounds like it's coming from the kitchen." She sounded frightened.

"Oh...okay," he said, fighting to clear his head. He turned away from Estelle and pushed back the bed blankets, trying to free himself. Then he swung his heavy legs over the side of the bed and sat for a moment before attempting to get out of bed. Once on his feet he walked quietly to the closet and slipped into his jeans. Foregoing shoes and a shirt to pull over the T-shirt he wore to bed, he moved into the dark hallway and paused, listening for any sound. He thought he heard the kitchen door close. Or was it only his imagination?

Still groggy, Fernando crept down the dark hallway past the living room. Suddenly he heard a car engine start out in his driveway. He moved quicker now, coming into the kitchen where he hit the wall switch and covered his eyes as bright light flooded the room, temporarily blinding him. When he could see again, he rushed to the window and looked out on his back yard. He saw a vehicle turning from his driveway onto Acequia Madre and disappearing behind the cottonwoods. Too dark to see the color or make of the vehicle.

Estelle was right to wake him. Someone had broken into their house while they were sleeping.

He looked around the kitchen, searching for damage. At first glance everything seemed to be in its proper place. Then he saw his cell phone charging cord dangling over the countertop, sans iphone. The sonofabitch had taken his cell phone, after using a lock pick to open the kitchen door. The identity of the intruder wasn't much of a mystery. It had to be either Cody or Snyder. Russo himself wouldn't stoop to petty thievery, even if he desperately wanted the Snake Dance video. Breaking and entering—that's what Russo had meant by 'other means' in his text message. That they were willing to break into his house to get what they wanted shouldn't come as much of a surprise. One of them had already killed at least one person.

The wall clock read 2:47 A.M. That meant Fernando had another three hours of much-needed sleep, if he could get back to sleep. So he shuffled down the hallway to his bedroom, removed his jeans, and crawled into bed with Estelle, who was waiting for him under the covers.

"What was it?" Estelle asked.

"Nothing," Fernando lied, not wanting to worry her. "Something fell from a shelf. I took care of it."

Estelle turned away from him and soon started snoring. She had an amazing ability to fall asleep instantly, whereas it often took Fernando hours to fall asleep, if he could fall asleep. Some nights sleep just wouldn't come unless he took one of his sleeping pills, which he hated. He tried his best to avoid taking them because they made his head feel stuffed full of cotton the next morning. A far cry from getting a good night's sleep.

Tossing and turning, Fernando dreamed of Roberto getting shot and falling on the floor of the dark La Fonda Parking Garage, his head bouncing off the concrete, while a hooded figure stood over him holding a smoking pistol. The reel played over and over in his sleep. Each time it played, more of the hooded figure's face was revealed so that Fernando could almost but never quite identify the hooded shooter standing over Roberto with a smoking gun.

Finally toward morning Estelle jumped out of the bed. "Maybe it's time we talk about different beds—or different bedrooms. Sleeping with you is like sleeping with a tornado. You need to take a sleeping pill or go back to the anxiety meds the shrink prescribed for you."

"Sorry, I'll take care of it," Fernando muttered, still groggy.

"That's what you say about everything," Estelle said. She threw up her hands in frustration and went into the bathroom.

Moments later Fernando heard the shower turn on. He managed to get out of bed, still half asleep, and pull on his jeans again. He shuffled barefoot down the hallway to the kitchen, deciding to make Estelle breakfast as a peace offering. He put the coffee on, scrambled some eggs with cheese and green chile, and had everything on the table when she came into the kitchen dressed for work.

"What's this? Again?" Estelle asked.

Well, it's the least I can do today—to make up for the rough night," Fernando replied.

After breakfast Estelle left for work right away, leaving Fernando alone to brood. He took a third cup of coffee and his cell phone out to the patio where he could enjoy the morning—a bright, clear day with a just a whiff of coolness in the air hinting at the coming fall.

He needed a plan of attack. Better to act quickly. The longer he waited, the more the risk of losing his cell phone irrevocably. He decided to again ask Blaine to accompany him, this time to the Film Collective. Blaine might be bat shit crazy, but he provided great back up and loved the challenge. Nothing pleased Blaine more than the pleasure of intimidating lesser mortals.

Fernando waited until half past nine before leaving. He locked the house and, after placing his Smith & Wessen in the glove compartment of the Cherokee, drove around to Blaine's Picasso and Co. Gallery on Canyon Road. He parked in the side lot and walked to the front door. When he opened the door, he found Tessa arranging Acoma pots on a shelf under a poster-sized black and white photo of Acoma Pueblo. Looked like a blown-up historical photo from the early Twentieth Century. Fernando loved Acoma pottery.

Tessa looked drop dead gorgeous and younger than ever, with her long black hair in a pony tail. Her short white shorts and slinky blue halter top brought back feelings Fernando hadn't felt since he'd spent some intimate time with her on his Death Demanded case.

"Where's Blaine?" he asked, trying to keep it official, not personal.

"He's in the back room exercising," Tessa said. "If you can call what he does 'exercising.'"

Fernando laughed. "I didn't know he exercised."

"Neither did I," Tessa replied, rolling her eyes.

Fernando waved and walked back into the office, spotting a small room off to the side that he hadn't noticed before. Through the open door he saw a rack of barbells and several mats on the floor. Blaine, dressed in his usual red Bermuda shorts and white T-shirt, was doing jumping jacks off to the side of the mats. Every few jumps he stopped to shadow box for a few seconds. He looked like a crazed Ernest Hemingway exercising between drinks.

Blaine stopped when Fernando stepped into the room. "What do you want?" he asked, grabbing a towel hanging from the barbell rack to wipe his sweaty face. Finished, Blaine tossed the towel back on the rack.

"I wanted to know if you were good for a little back-up again today," Fernando said. "I know how much you love it."

Blaine smiled. "Who is it? The same dumb fucks?"

Fernando nodded. "The same dumb fucks."

"Sure...just let me get dressed," Blaine said. He disappeared into their rear living quarters and then came back a minute or so later wearing exactly the same thing except for the addition of his khaki fishing vest.

"Yeah, you're a real quick change artist, all right," Fernando quipped.

Blaine gave him a dirty look.

Fernando led the way, with Blaine following after he'd grabbed Tessa and given her a long wet kiss.

"Wait for me...I don't want to miss the fun," the big man said to Fernando, running to catch up.

Fernando drove around the Paseo to Old Santa Fe Trail and up to the Santa Fe Armory for the Arts. Once he'd parked and killed the engine, Fernando told Blaine about the break-in at his house last night and his missing cell phone.

Blaine couldn't believe it. "You mean, you let these guys break into your house and steal your cell phone? What the fuck?"

"I was asleep," Fernando said in his defense.

"So what, you have a security system, don't you," Blaine replied. "The last time someone broke into my gallery he left with a concussion and two broken ribs. I didn't press charges because he was just a homeless guy down on his luck, but I told the sonofabitch that if he ever tried to rob my place again I would break even more of his fucking ribs."

Fernando nodded. "Let's do this."

Fernando led the way, marching down the long hallway up to the door of the Santa Fe Film Collective. A couple of other people in the hallway noticed Fernando's agitation and moved away, keeping their distance. No one spoke.

Fernando was a man on a mission.

Blaine grabbed Fernando's arm at the door of the film collective. "Just remember: you go in fast, you get what you want, and you leave fast. Never back track, always move forward."

With that, Fernando opened the door and kicked it with such force that it smashed into the wall, cracking the plaster.

22

Wes Snyder froze at his computer, looking across his desk with a look of hatred on his face. He looked like he was about to come unglued. He opened his mouth but nothing came out.

Fernando stormed into the inner office, leaving Blaine standing with his hands on both sides of the door jamb, blocking the way in or out of the office complex.

Fernando stopped in the center of the office glaring at Russo, who sat quietly at his desk looking over a spreadsheet. Russo glanced at Fernando nonchalantly and then back to his spreadsheet, seemingly unaffected by the disruption. Calm, cool, and collected, the man was absolutely imperturbable. Above it all.

"Where's my cell phone?" Fernando demanded.

Russo pointed to the corner of his desk. "Help yourself."

Fernando grabbed the phone and stuffed it in his pocket.

"Now we both have what we wanted," Russo said, smiling.

"Not exactly," Fernando said. "I want you to stop making the movie. It's a desecration, a violation of Hopi religion and culture."

Russo shook his head. "Wrong. I'm not making the movie, I'm simply procuring a property for the people who are making the movie. That's what we do here—we provide services."

Fernando took a seat in the chair facing Russo's desk. "Yeah, but you have to understand that Durand just wants to use snippets from the Snake Dance video to exploit its sensational properties...for profit."

Russo laughed. "Come on, Lopez, we're living in end-stage capitalism, run by thieves and con men. There's nothing left but sensationalism and titillation. Look at the movies being shown in the theaters these days, look at mainstream culture, nothing but violent video games and movies, all to maximize profit. The only values today are money and power. If Durand doesn't make that movie, someone else will, don't you understand?"

"So your nihilism is all we're left with," Fernando replied.

"Call it what you will," Russo shot back. "The exploiters have drained the meaning out of everything. There's nothing left but an empty, vapid culture where only the bottom line matters: profit!"

Fernando found it difficult to argue with Russo because he agreed with much of what the man said. Unfortunately.

"Yeah, I suppose, but we don't have to participate in this exploitation... this destruction of Hopi religion and culture. We have a choice."

Russo shrugged. "Up to you. But if you don't participate, you're not in the game. You're not a player. That comes with a price too."

Fernando had heard enough. He stood to leave when he saw Snyder coming into the inner office.

"Just remember—your house is easy to get into," Snyder said disdainfully, a cruel smile on his face.

The smile infuriated Fernando. "You!" he shouted and rushed at Snyder. Grabbing Snyder by his shirt, he spun the smug punk around and shoved him hard into the bookshelf along the wall. Books and files cascaded over Snyder, who continued smiling at Fernando, mocking him.

Furious now, Fernando grabbed Snyder around the neck and started choking him. Only Blaine, bursting in the room just then, prevented Fernando from doing something he would regret.

"Let him go, he's not worth it," Blaine said, prying Fernando's hands off Snyder who fell back into the bookcase and then slithered down on the floor, where he continued to smile at the two men standing over him.

"You come near my house again—I'll kill you," Fernando spit out.

Snyder laughed at that.

"Come on," Blaine said, pulling Fernando away from Snyder before he could react to Snyder's taunts.

Blaine pulled and then shoved Fernando into the outer office and then outside into the hallway. "Turn your goddamn security system on, okay?" he said to Fernando. "Then you won't have any problems."

As they walked down the hallway Fernando began to cool off. Blind rage gave way to thoughts of revenge. The sonofabitch had broken into his house, while he and Estelle were in bed. As Blaine said, he would need to activate his security system every night before turning in.

Fernando had changed his mind. He now believed Russo. Snyder had gunned down Roberto in the La Fonda Parking Garage, not Cody. He should never have doubted Russo's reliability.

He saw it clearly now: Snyder's cruelty.

When they reached the end of the hallway and opened the front door of the Armory, Fernando swore he could hear Snyder laughing behind them.

"Don't worry about him, he's just a punk," Blaine said as he escorted Fernando across the parking lot to the Cherokee. "He has a smart mouth but nothing else. Believe me, he's not worth killing. Let someone else have that honor. With a mouth like that, it shouldn't take long."

Now Fernando laughed. He was being cautioned to stay calm by the most volatile, belligerent person he'd ever known. Talk about irony.

23

After he dropped off Blaine at Picasso and Co. on Canyon Road, Fernando drove downtown and parked on Marcy Street next to the coffee shop. He needed another cup of coffee to clear his head and to forget what had just gone down at the Santa Fe Film Collective's office. He bought two coffees to go, one for himself and one for Manny. Then he carried the coffees around the corner and down the block to the Washington Avenue Station.

He found the same young redheaded woman with glasses behind the front counter when he walked into the station. She smiled at him and pointed down the hallway. "I know who you are now," she said.

Fernando didn't know if that was good or bad, but he raised one of his coffees and thanked her.

"Manny," Fernando announced when he stepped into his office, "I brought you coffee!"

Manny looked up from his desk, still cluttered with stacks of papers and folders. "Yeah? What's the occasion?"

"Just thought you might need one as much as I do this morning," Fernando said, handing Manny one of the steaming paper cups of coffee. "You like it black, as I recall, right?"

Manny nodded. The usually dapper little man looked tired, with dark circles under his eyes and days-old stubble on his face.

"Jesus, you're hair's sticking up like a goddamn porcupine's," Fernando said, laughing as he took a seat facing Manny's desk. "Rough week?"

"Aren't they all?" Manny replied. "You should have warned me."

"Hey—I tried," Fernando said. "So what's new in the shooting of the guy in the La Fonda Parking Garage?"

"Roberto Mendoza," Manny said. "We brought Cody in for questioning, but he had a solid alibi, so we're pretty much back to square one."

"For what it's worth, Max Russo told me Wes Snyder killed Roberto," Fernando said. "I have reason to believe he's right."

"You mean the little guy in the Film Collective's front office?" Manny asked.

Fernando nodded. "He's not so little...and he's mean as a snake. Take my word for it."

"Well, we can bring him in for questioning...." Manny started, but trailed off. He sounded skeptical.

Fernando pried off the top of his cup of coffee and took a long drink and then another.

Manny did the same but let the open cup of coffee set. He sighed. "I don't know how you did it for all those years. I got cases piling up on me faster than I can clear them. I can't keep up—it's impossible with the short staff we have. Then this morning I got a call from the Hopi Tribal Police Chief," Manny said, shaking his head.

"Hopi?" Fernando asked.

Manny nodded. "He wanted me to stop the movie they're making down at Bonanza Creek Ranch. Wanted me to stop the movie and arrest the director and everyone else responsible. As if I had the power to do that—or even wanted to do it if I had the power."

"So what did you tell him?" Fernando asked.

"Just that," Manny said. "I told him I had no authority to shut down the movie and suggested he try to get an injunction, a court order to stop the movie. I said I was skeptical he could find a judge, but that it was worth a try."

Fernando shook his head. "Not going to happen."

"I know, but I had to tell him something, right? The Hopi are the only ones with standing. Legal action has to originate from them. I know it's a long-shot."

Manny took a long drink from his coffee. He set the coffee cup back on his desk. "Then he told me the Snake Clan was sending a delegation of its members to help arrest the guilty parties. Apparently, they're on their way to Santa Fe as we speak. Can you believe that? Help arrest?"

"Wait? What do they expect to accomplish?" Fernando asked.

"To help arrest the guilty parties, like I said."

Now Fernando was worried. "Have you told anyone else about this?"

"Yeah, I called Jodie right after I got off the phone with the Hopi," Manny replied. "It's her jurisdiction out there, she's going to have to deal with the situation if these people do arrive. She was pissed, as you can imagine. She's even shorter staffed than I am. And shorter tempered."

"What about the Chief? Have you told him?" Fernando asked.

Manny laughed. "The Chief? You have to be kidding. That's the last goddamn thing the Chief wants to hear, believe me."

Fernando didn't know what to say, so he said nothing.

Manny threw up his arms. "So I don't know what the fuck's gonna happen. No idea."

24

Leaving the Washington Avenue Station Fernando began to worry about Manny. The usually upbeat, jocular Manny seemed positively overwhelmed by developments. From thirty years of experience in that office he knew Manny had more than enough on his plate. The last thing Manny needed was this movie debacle and the threat of a Hopi invasion.

Fernando drove back to his house on Acequia Madre Street. He planned to take the rest of the day off to relax. After the early morning break-in and his confrontation with Max Russo and the Film Collective yahoos, he hadn't slept a wink. Now that he had his cell phone back, he'd lost the urge to do much of anything other than sit on his patio and hide from trouble. He'd had his share of trouble today, thank you.

Once inside, the house seemed eerily calm, after the morning turmoil. He made himself a light lunch and took it outside to the patio, his place of refuge. As he relaxed, he felt his body begin to release its tension. Eventually his eyelids began to droop. He decided to do something he almost never did: take an afternoon nap. So he went back inside and lay down on the living room sofa, after placing his cell phone on the coffee table.

Fernando fell immediately into a deep sleep, the sleep of the dead. No dreams, no nightmares, nothing. When the ringing of his cell phone awoke him, he was shocked to see the time. Nearly four o'clock. He'd been asleep on the sofa for several hours. He never slept on the sofa.

His spirits sank when he picked up the phone and saw the name, Jodie Williams. What now? Against his better judgment he clicked accept.

"Fernando...all hell's breaking loose down here at the Bonanza Creek Ranch," Jodie said. She sounded stressed. Big time.

"What do you mean?" Fernando asked.

"The Hopi Snake Clan arrived this afternoon," Jodie said. "They know about the stolen video. They want the video destroyed and the production of 'The Lower World' stopped."

"Manny told me they were coming. How did they find about the video?" Fernando asked.

"Apparently they saw Jeff Walker shooting the video," Jodie replied. "Can you come down and talk to them? You're the only person with a copy of the video. We're on the verge of another Indian war and I'm the fucking U.S. Calvary, me and one of my deputies."

Fernando ignored Jodie's last sentence. "Well, I also sent a copy of the video to Manny," Fernando said, omitting the copy that Russo purloined from Fernando's cell phone last night.

"That's fine, but this is out of Manny's jurisdiction...and you are the source of all these copies, understand?"

"Cowboys and Indians," Fernando mumbled to himself, copying what Jodie had just said.

"What?"

"Never mind...I'm on my way," Fernando said, clicking off.

Before putting aside his cell phone, Fernando took a moment to email another copy of the video to himself. That way he would be sure of having a copy, just in case he lost his cell phone in a struggle at Bonanza Creek Ranch or if his cell phone was somehow confiscated. He wanted to make sure he had a copy of the video for future litigation, if it came to that.

He knew from experience what the Hopi would do if and when they learned he had a copy of the video. They would take a look at it and then make him delete it in their presence. He'd had this happen to him while taking photos at several Pueblos over the years: Santo Domingo, Taos, Zuni, to name a few. If you take a photo of a prohibited area or function, they will keep you company until you delete the forbidden image or video. They'd even been known to confiscate cameras.

Finished with the email, Fernando drove up Alameda to the Paseo and took it to Old Santa Fe Trail. Then he shot up to Interstate 25 and raced down to Bonanza Creek Road. Took him less than fifteen minutes to reach the ranch. He stopped at the gate to get his breath. He closed his eyes and meditated for a moment, trying to relax. After a few minutes he felt ready, or as ready as he would ever be, so he started the big engine and hit the gas pedal. Show time.

Bouncing down the dirt road to the office he saw something that looked right out of a movie: a crowd of people running from the office to the Mountain Cabin set, where René Durand's 'The Lower World' was shooting. He followed behind the angry crowd, poking along slowly to avoid hitting anyone. Everyone seemed to be shouting at once, so that all the angry words blended together in a dull roar.

Coming into one turn he came too close and nicked one burly crew member who pounded on the side of the Cherokee and then started on the side windows. Fernando feared the windows would pop, which prompted him to slow down to a crawl. Finally he found himself stopping and starting, inching forward.

Up ahead in the parking area Fernando spotted Jodie's cruiser and a scattering of other vehicles and trailers. One in particular caught his interest, a dusty yellow Ford Transit with three rows of seats. The massive vehicle had Arizona license plates and no doubt belonged to the Hopis who'd come to retrieve or destroy the stolen video of their Snake Dance and to stop production of the movie.

When the crowd thinned, Fernando managed to park beside Jodie's cruiser and climb out of the Cherokee. He didn't know where to start. Next to the trailers he saw René Durand's Mini. Durand paced back and forth behind the Mini with hands over his ears to drown out the angry shouting on the trail up to the mesa, where the crowd seemed to have gathered.

Ignoring Durand, Fernando started for the trail into the crowd. Everyone seemed to be pushing forward to the front of the scram—film crew members, office workers, even some of the actors in partial costume, as if they'd been dragged out of their trailers while dressing for the night's shoot, which was scheduled to start any minute now as far as Fernando could tell. The light was draining fast out of the eastern sky, while the western horizon flamed orange and crimson.

He spotted Jodie and one of her deputies up on the trail. The deputy waved his arms at the crowd, trying to keep the rowdies off the trail, while Jodie stood talking to one of Durand's gaffers, a tall bean-pole of a man with a gray goatee who Fernando had seen earlier. Surrounding them were several members of what Fernando assumed was the Hopi Snake

Clan. The Hopis wore jeans and colorful cotton shirts, with beaded belts around their shirts. The oldest, with a feather tucked into his headband, stood nearest to Jodie and the gaffer, speaking to them in a calm, deliberate manner that contrasted with the melee in the parking lot that had grown more intense now. People were pushing and shoving and yelling at one another. A fist fight had started over by the Ford Transit, a couple of Hopis versus several members of what looked like the film crew. Punches were exchanged and seconds later all of them were on the ground wrestling and cursing one another.

"Out of my way!" a big man behind Fernando barked and shoved him off the trail. Fernando stumbled and came close to falling down the hill for the second time. He fell on his hands and knees and managed to stop the slide, producing a shower of stones rolling down the hill.

Why the hurry? What was happening at the top of the mesa?

25

Everyone started shouting at once, creating a deafening roar. Through the noise and the mayhem Fernando managed to get back on his feet. When he did, he spotted Jodie waving at him from the flat ledge along the trail further down toward the parking area. She waved for him to come down, so he headed back down the trail against the oncoming crowd, getting damn tired of being jostled from one side of the trail to the other.

"Fernando, this is Tuvi, he's from the Hopi Snake Dance Clan at Walpi, Jodie said as he approached the flat ledge. "He wants to stop the movie production."

Fernando nodded. He had no idea how Tuvi or anyone else planned to stop the production.

"Tuvi, this is Fernando, the man I was telling you about," Jodie said, turning to the elder. "He has a copy of the video."

Staring at Fernando, Tuvi said, "You steal our Snake Dance." His voice was matter of fact, without emotion.

"No, I didn't steal it, but I have a copy of the dance on my cell phone that I took from the person who did steal it," Fernando replied.

The bean-pole gaffer's face turned red. He stroked his gray goatee, furious at Fernando.

Tuvi held out his hand.

Fernando took out his cell phone and booted up the video. Then he handed it to Tuvi, who watched for a couple of minutes and then handed the cell phone back to Fernando.

"We must erase," Tuvi said finally.

"I know. Here, let me erase it," Fernando said, using Tuvi's word.

"No! Wait!" the gaffer said, grabbing for the cell phone.

Jodie knocked the gaffer's hand away and said, "Stay out of this." Then she moved between him and Fernando.

"Idiots!" the gaffer said.

Ignoring the gaffer, Fernando clicked the delete button and then showed Tuvi the video had been deleted.

Tuvi turned to his fellow Snake Clan members and spoke to them in the Hopi language, a unique and very complex Uto-Aztecan language that was difficult to understand. Fernando didn't have a clue. Neither did Jodie or the gaffer or anyone else in hearing distance, other than the Hopis. All of them waited until Tuvi had finished speaking.

When he finished, Tuvi and the other Hopis turned and headed up the trail toward the film set on top of the mesa.

"Stop them! They'll harm the set!" the gaffer yelled. He was jumping up and down now, waving at his crew below in the parking lot. "Hurry! We have to save the set!"

With that, the gaffer dashed around Jodie and started running up the trail. He stumbled and fell to his knees for a moment and then scrambled back on his feet and continued running. He caught and grabbed one of the Hopis who'd fallen behind the others, a plump middle-aged man with a long ponytail. "Ay-ee," the Hopi exclaimed, as the two men fell to the ground, rolling down the side of the hill wrestling in the sparse grass.

By this time everyone in the parking lot had charged up the trail, swarming around and past Jodie and Fernando who tried in vain to hold them back. The crowd stampeded by like a herd of buffalo. Fernando had no idea if they wanted to protect or destroy the set. Probably both.

Cursing, and tired of being pushed and shoved, Fernando stepped off the trail and let them pass. Jodie did the same.

"Where's Scott?" Jodie asked.

Fernando pointed to the bottom of the trail, where Jodie's deputy sat on his ass in a patch of prickly pear cactus. Scott got to his feet gingerly and began picking cactus needles out of his ass and legs. "Fuck!" Scott shouted every time he pulled a needle out of his flesh.

Shaking her head, Jodie started up the trail. Fernando followed. Neither of them was in any hurry to reach the top, where everyone seemed to be cursing and shouting angrily.

As they approached the movie set they saw the gaffer with a bloody nose jumping up and down and running around like a chicken with its head cut off. They saw why momentarily. The Hopis were kicking and ripping the canvas backdrop off its two-by-four frame, leaving only strips of torn and tattered canvas flapping in the wind. Meanwhile, other members of the Snake Dance Clan knocked over the partial adobe walls on either side of the fake kiva. In their fury they tossed and scattered the broken adobes over the entire area.

Some of the crew members made halfhearted attempts to put the adobe wall back again, arranging the broken pieces. Others tried to gather what remained of the canvas backdrop and refasten it to its frame, but the Hopis just ripped it down as fast as the crew members refastened it. The result was a set that had a blown-apart look more appropriate for a war movie.

Finally the Hopis gathered at the fake kiva and started laughing at the rubber snakes deposited there. One of them grabbed a rubber snake and started swinging it over his head like a lariat. Several other Hopis soon joined him. Then the lot of them started a mock dance, prancing around the dusty mesa whirling the rubber snakes over their heads and laughing.

Trashed. The only word that came to Fernando's mind as he looked over the ruins of the set. The set would have to be entirely rebuilt, starting with a new canvas painted and then attached to its wooden frame and new adobes for the partial walls on either side. They would even need a new supply of rubber snakes after some of the Hopis began cutting up the snakes with their knives and setting fire to them in the bottom of the fake kiva. A total wipe-out.

Eventually the Hopis left the mutilated rubber snakes to burn and began making their way back down the trail in no particular hurry. They'd accomplished what they intended to do, which was to destroy the movie set. When they reached the bottom of the trail, they gathered around their Ford Transit and waited for Tuvi, who was now in an animated conversation with René Durand. Tuvi talked with his arms open and outstretched, while Durand jumped up and down and gestured wildly with his hands, no doubt going on and on about the artistic merits of the film. After all, Durand was a master at masking greed as art. It was clear the two of them did not see eye to eye, which wasn't surprising since one spoke Hopi and the other spoke French and it would be damn hard to find a translator fluent in both Hopi and French in Santa Fe where most folks spoke Spanish and Spanglish.

While Fernando watched from the top of the mesa the Hopis, taking their good time, climbed into their Ford Transit and drove off slowly, honking at anyone who got in their way. One office worker had to jump in the ditch to avoid being hit by the Transit. He jumped back up and flashed his middle finger at the big Ford, which continued on down the drive in no particular hurry.

Fernando turned his attention to the bloody gaffer, who now that the war had been fought and lost, took a seat on a portion of the broken adobe wall and tried to clean up his bloody nose. The gaffer took a handkerchief out of his back pocket and started dabbing at the blood on his face, managing only to smear his entire face with blood. He snarled when he saw Fernando approach.

"Fucking savages," the gaffer said.

"Watch what you say," Fernando responded. "We don't like that kind of talk around here. The Hopi have been here for thousands of years. They're an ancient culture that deserves respect."

"Oh, piss off! Leave me alone," the gaffer said, frowning.

By this time most of the crew members and actors had disembarked, walking back down the trail to the parking lot. An eerie silence had descended on the trashed movie set, with bits and pieces of canvas still flapping in the wind and dust from the broken adobes gusting in the wind and forming little dust devils that whirled through the carnage.

The entire top of the mesa looked like the aftermath of a natural disaster, a tornado or an earthquake maybe. Nothing left but silence among the ruins. Desolation row.

Jodie walked over to join them. She looked down at the scowling gaffer. "See what you've caused? What were you thinking?"

Again the gaffer said, "Leave me alone."

Jodie shook her head and walked away. Fernando followed her down the trail to the parking lot, where Scott leaned against the cruiser, waiting for Jodie. He'd apparently picked the last of the cactus needles out of his ass.

"We haven't seen the last of this," Jodie said.

Fernando stood back and watched as Jodie and Scott talked to people from the Bonanza Creek Ranch office for a few minutes before climbing into their cruiser and slamming their doors shut as if they were angry. He had no idea what the conversation involved or what they had decided, if anything.

Fernando watched Jodie's cruiser drive off, following in the tracks of the Ford Transit. Then he spotted René Durand sitting in his Mini by himself with his side widow halfway down. With his head bowed, Durand appeared to be sleeping or maybe meditating.

"You okay?" Fernando asked, coming closer.

Durand turned to look at him and then buzzed up the window.

26

Next day Fernando spent the morning tending to his bumps and bruises. The riot at Bonanza Creek Ranch had been an eye-opening experience. Last night's brawl had shattered the illusion of cultural détente. The differences were just too vast to bridge. Max Russo was right, it came down to a question of values. For mainstream European culture—end-stage capitalism, as Russo called it—the only value was profit. Some Europeans paid lip service to the fantasy of organized religion, but it was all pretense if you looked at how they actually behaved, how they lived their lives. On the other hand the Hopis and Pueblos and other Native American tribes valued their sacred traditions as well as the natural world that provided their home. For Europeans the planet was just something to dig up and spit out as cash, fuck the consequences. That was what Fernando thought anyway. He'd gone to the dark side.

Last night the Hopis had won a temporary victory. They'd managed to destroy the movie set and at least temporarily postpone the movie production. Beyond that, who knew?

After lunch, Fernando went for a long walk on Acequia Madre Street. When he returned, he went into his study and looked for a book he'd read years ago, *Book of the Hopi* by Southwestern writer Frank Waters. He found it on the same shelf he once kept D.H. Lawrence's *Mornings in Mexico*. After revisiting the Snake Dance he was curious to know more about the Hopi. He'd read the book years ago at about the same time he'd read the Lawrence book. As soon as he sat down at his desk and began reading, he began to remember. The Hopi are a matrilineal society organized by clan membership, matrilineal meaning the Hopi trace their families through their mothers. The major clans are the Bear, Parrot,

Eagle, Badger, Spider, Fire, Snake, Water, Pumpkin, Bow, Black Seed, and Coyote clans. The society is highly ceremonial, arranged around nine religious ceremonies that roughly complement the solar cycles. Sitting at his desk he reread the parts about the Snake Clan and its annual dances. Once again he was amazed at the intricacies of Hopi ceremonialism, how seriously Hopi traditions and religion were followed.

After he finished reading about the Snake Clan, Fernando decided he needed to get out of the house, just get away from his troubles for a while. He checked the time, nearly four o'clock. That meant Happy Hour at El Farol was just beginning. Perfect timing.

He locked up the house and drove around to Canyon Road and up to El Farol. He parked in the lot across the street and walked over to the El Farol porch, where a couple of young women were sitting at a table drinking pink concoctions and, from what he heard, comparing tales about their "lame-ass" boyfriends.

Inside Fernando found the bar empty, unusual for El Farol, one of the most popular watering holes in Santa Fe. Most of his Canyon Road friends were in the restaurant part of El Farol, sitting at tables along the rear wall near the colorful mural of Flamenco dancers. Ruby and the other regulars sat at the table nearest the mural, Blaine and Tessa, even Dave Stein and June Bryan. Only Paul Bryan, June's husband, was missing.

Ruby waved him over. "Have a seat, Fernando. Join the crowd. We're celebrating."

"Celebrating what?" Fernando asked.

"I can't remember," Ruby said, holding up her margarita. By the sound of her voice, she'd started Happy Hour early today.

Fernando sat next to Ruby, across the table from Blaine and Tessa, who were feeding each other corn chips dipped in salsa. At least they weren't smooching or arguing, which they were usually doing, one or the other.

Dave Stein sat with June Bryan on another side of the table, a rarity because June rarely appeared without Paul, her husband.

"Where's Paul?" Fernando asked, sitting beside Ruby.

June made a face. "We're on the outs. I caught him with some floozy in the massage room yesterday. He was doing massage where he shouldn't be doing massage—with his tongue!"

Everyone laughed.

"Damn, I didn't think Paul even had a libido," Ruby said. "I mean, talk about squeaky clean and button-down, Paul's your man?"

"True," Blaine added, turning to June. "Hard to believe a man like that could ever satisfy you, June. You have needs. I know from experience."

Tessa sputtered "What?" and elbowed Blaine in the side.

"Ouch!" Blaine cried out. "That's my fucking liver!"

"What's left of it," Tessa replied.

Ruby shook her head and waved her hands at Blaine and Tessa, as if trying to magically make them disappear.

"So Manny found out who killed Gail?" Ruby asked Fernando.

Fernando nodded. "Apparently it was Roberto Mendoza, one of the director René Durand's team. They found his fingerprints all over Gail's house. Then Wes Snyder of the Santa Fe Film Collective gunned down Roberto in the La Fonda Parking Garage. At least that's what we think."

"Jesus— that's three people dead because of the damn Snake Dance video," Ruby replied.

"Four, if you count Jeff Walker," Fernando replied.

"So what's the latest on the movie?" Ruby asked. "I heard there was trouble on the set yesterday."

Fernando laughed. "I guess. Members of the Hopi Snake Clan arrived and started raising hell. Then it turned into a full-scale riot, with the Hopi fighting with the film crew and the Bonanza Creek Ranch staff. The film set was completely destroyed in the fighting. I mean completely. There was nothing left after the Hopi finished their work. So the movie production has been stopped—at least temporarily."

"I heard. I guess that's why they're moving production down to Albuquerque," Ruby said.

Fernando, puzzled, asked, "What do you mean?"

"Do you know Anne Romero, one of the ladies in my pottery co-op?" Ruby asked. "Well, her two sons are working as extras in that movie, 'The Lower World.' She said both of them are pissing and moaning about having to drive down to Albuquerque for the production, after it was moved to Albuquerque Studios this morning. She said they have better security there to keep out the troublemakers and lots of space. I think she said five hundred thousand square feet."

"No kidding?"

"Production resumes tomorrow." Ruby replied.

Fernando shook his head sadly. "This is news to me. So the exploitation will continue, after all."

Ruby glared at Fernando. "Of course. Anything to make a dirty dollar. What did you expect?"

Fernando sighed. "Yeah, that's pretty much what I expected, although I thought it might take longer than a day for them to get started again. So where is Albuquerque Studios?"

"Anne said it was south of the university on the southern edge of the city, past the Sunport at the very end of University Boulevard," Ruby replied. "That's all I know about it, other than Anne's sons are supposed to report first thing tomorrow morning. Unlike everyone else in the state, I'm not head over heels in love with the damn film industry. Let's not forget tourism—and arts and crafts."

"Like pottery?" Fernando joked.

"Well yeah," Ruby said. "Name one movie filmed here that's made big money for the state."

"How about the 'Milagro Beanfield War'?" Fernando asked.

Ruby shrugged. "I said big money. So anyway 'The Lower World' production is gonna go undercover. They'll make the movie and then just spring it on us. The Hopi better have their lawyer ready."

"I imagine they will," Fernando replied. "They're not passive, as we saw yesterday."

While they talked, a young server who Fernando hadn't seen before walked over to the table. "What can I get you?" she asked Fernando, a petite blonde with a nose ring and tattoos on both arms.

"Modelo draft."

She smiled. "I think I saw a photo of you somewhere. Maybe in the daily newspaper?"

"Probably," Fernando said. "I used to be a Santa Fe Police Detective."

"Oh...I'm sorry to hear that," she said and walked away.

What did she mean by that, Fernando wondered. Sorry?

Moments later she returned with the Modelo and smiled again. Was she flirting with him? He found it impossible to understand young people these days.

"So it sounds like we'll never know if Jeff Walker's death was an accident or a murder," Ruby said, redirecting Fernando's attention. "That was what started all this mess."

Fernando nodded. "Probably not. I don't think the Arizona State Police are all that interested in investigating the crash—or finding out who else could be involved in the crash."

"Who do you mean?" Ruby asked.

"The Hopis...other people associated with the movie, who knows," Fernando said.

"Maybe it's better we don't know," Ruby added.

"We do what we can," Fernando said, talking to himself now, resigned.

Soon Blaine and Tessa started arguing about how and when to open a joint show at his Picasso and Co. Gallery, which prompted Fernando and Ruby to order another drink and then one more for the road as the long day's journey ticked inexorably into night.

27

A car engine starting outside in his driveway woke Fernando. He looked at the other side of the bed, which was empty, and then at the bedside clock. Half past seven o'clock. Estelle was leaving for work early and he was still in bed. He took a moment to clear his head, still foggy from one too many Modelo drafts last night. He should have come home earlier. Shoulda... shoulda...lotta things he shoulda done differently in his sixty years. Too late to make amends now.

He climbed out of bed and dressed, taking his time. He had nothing on his plate this morning, now that 'The Lower World' movie production had moved down the road to Albuquerque. Good riddance to all those involved. He wanted to forget everyone involved in this sorry episode, René Durand as well as Max Russo and his co-conspirators at the Santa Fe Film Collective.

Instead, he thought he would drive out to the Pecos Wilderness to check on Antonio Blake's cabin. He'd received an email from his old friend and colleague at the Santa Fe Police Department last night saying that he would be coming down to Santa Fe for Fiesta next week. Antonio had retired a couple of years ago and moved to Colorado to help his son manage a ranch near Alamosa, a ranch that his son had inherited from his maternal grandparents. Fernando hadn't heard much from Antonio since he'd left Pecos and was eager to catch up with his old friend. He wanted to make sure Antonio's cabin hadn't been vandalized or taken over by four-legged squatters, the animals that prowled the Pecos Wilderness day and night.

In the kitchen he found a pot of cold coffee, which he poured into the sink. Then he made himself a fresh cup of coffee in his Keurig and took it out on the patio. The thought of Antonio returning for a visit cheered him. He missed Antonio. They'd been inseparable for years, through good times and bad. After he finished his coffee, he went back into the house to make a second cup. While the Keurig clicked and hissed, his cell phone rang on the kitchen counter. He saw the name on the screen immediately: Manny Alvarez. He'd texted Manny last night after Antonio's email arrived. The three of them were old friends.

"What's up, Manny?" Fernando answered.

"Got your text—just checking in with you," Manny said. "We're free down here. Durand and that fucking movie moved down to Albuquerque. We no longer have to deal with them—or the Hopis."

"I heard," Fernando replied.

"Both Jodie and I are relieved, I can't tell you," Manny continued. "I thought we were going to have another race war out there at Bonanza Creek Ranch. The Hopis were really pissed."

"At least they weren't armed," Fernando added.

Manny laughed. "Thank God."

"Did you contact the Albuquerque PD to give them a head's up?" Fernando asked.

"I tried," Manny replied. "They weren't particularly interested, said they'd take care of it, like they always do. Same old arrogance we always get from them. Like they're so much better than we are."

"Just bigger," Fernando said. "By the way, what's the latest on the Roberto Mendoza shooting?"

Manny sighed. "Not much. We know about the feud between Roberto and the Film Collective people, but again we're getting blowback from the Chief and the Mayor. Both of them are trying to put a lid on the investigation—they want us to move on so as not to reflect badly on the fucking film industry. Same old same old."

"Yeah...I sympathize," Fernando said. "At least you don't have to worry about the movie."

"True, that," Manny said. "So give me a call when you hear more about Antonio's visit. Maybe the three of us can do a little Fiesta celebrating, like the good old days. Although I don't think I can drink as much as I did back then," Manny said, laughing.

"I'd like that," Fernando said.

Manny clicked off and left Fernando holding his cell phone. "Later," he mumbled to himself.

He took his coffee back out to the patio. Sitting on his favorite bench he couldn't stop brooding about the one thing Manny said that bothered him: the likelihood that Wes Snyder would not be held accountable for the murder of Roberto. Didn't set well with him. The smell of it lingered, so to speak. That Snyder could gun down Roberto in the La Fonda Parking Garage and walk away without facing any consequences. What about justice?

The longer he sat on the patio, the more he felt obligated to do something, anything to punish Wes Snyder. Finally he made a decision. He would drive down to Albuquerque Studios and confront Snyder, let him know that he, Fernando, knew he had killed Roberto. Put him on notice, so that he had to watch over his shoulder twenty-four-seven. That might be the best he could do under the circumstances.

That settled, he waited until after lunch to strap on the holster holding his Smith & Wesson, which would be good for show, if nothing else. Then he grabbed a couple bottles of water from their refrigerator and walked out to his Cherokee. He drove around the Paseo to Old Santa Fe Trail and headed for Interstate-25. Once on the interstate he drove fast, much faster than he would normally. He wanted to get this over as quickly as possible.

Fernando hated the sixty-mile drive to Albuquerque. Not even Santa Domingo and San Felipe pueblos made the drive bearable. Partly it was the traffic speeding down La Bajada Hill. Everyone drove like a motherfucker these days, like they were racing the Devil or the Grim Reaper himself. Then the consumer crap on the outskirts of Albuquerque came into sight, mucking up his views of the Sandia and Monzano mountains. Ugly.

He followed I-25 south through Albuquerque and took the exit to the Sunport, the name of Albuquerque's airport. Instead of taking the road to the Sunport, he followed University Boulevard south to Albuquerque Studios, a scattering of enormous tan buildings surrounded by what looked like a cement block wall. At one end of the sprawling compound he found a parking lot and pulled in under the overhead gate with "Albuquerque" written in big black letters.

After parking, Fernando walked into the compound, looking for signs that would direct him to the studio where 'The Lower World' was being filmed. He found a billboard where the various productions and their locations were listed. Turned out that Durand and his team were shooting at Stage 4, which he located on the billboard map. One of the smaller buildings.

He walked into the compound, following the signs to Stage 4, where he spotted Durand's trailers behind the building. He also spotted the Ford Transit that he'd seen at Bonanza Creek Ranch. Sure enough, Tuvi and his Snake Clan followers had followed the production to Albuquerque. They marched in front of the doors of Stage 4 holding make-shift signs with crude slogans painted in red paint that seemed to bleed off the posters: 'End Colonialism!', 'Hands off Hopi Religion!', 'Stop Stealing Hopi Snake Dance!', and so on.

Between the demonstrators and the doors of the building stood a line of six or seven Albuquerque Police officers in full riot gear. They stood stony-faced, wearing sunglasses, staring blankly at the protestors who chanted and berated them nonstop. In contrast to the animated demonstrators, the officers looked bored, as though they'd been through too many of these mundane protests that changed nothing. Been there, done that, seemed to be their attitude.

Tuvi waved to him as Fernando made his way through the members of the Snake Dance Clan. He ignored Tuvi and walked up to an older officer with a gray goatee whose badge read Rodriguez, who stared blankly at him, showing no emotion.

"Howdy," Fernando said in as friendly a voice as he could muster at the moment. "I'm helping with movie security," he said, not exactly the truth but close enough, he figured. He took out his wallet and showed Rodriguez his business card listing him as a private investigator and former Santa Fe Police Detective.

Rodriguez nodded and motioned for Fernando to go on through.

"Thanks," Fernando said, walking confidently through the police line and into the building.

Inside, he saw different stages off a long hallway leading back to a fairly large gathering of people. Looked like Durand's crew and assorted actors, getting ready for a shoot. They didn't have to wait until the evening here, because lighting was carefully controlled inside each of the studios. One click of a switch and it would be night or day, depending on what the script called for. Everything was artificial here—pure artifice. Even the spinning of the earth. Fake.

Fernando walked cautiously toward the group, not sure how he would be received after Roberto's murder. For all he knew, they might blame him for the shooting. As he came closer he saw the studio had the same look as the canvas backdrop back at Bonanza Creek Ranch. In fact, the canvas was identical, with the same building painted on the canvas and partial adobe walls on either side of the canvas. A shallow kiva in front completed the design. The set was constructed on a platform, with a wooden ramp up built to resemble a rocky mesa trail leading up to the platform. The platform served as a plaza where the dancers would appear and grab their snakes from the kiva.

He found Durand conversing with two men carrying clipboards. Maybe it took two of them to replace Roberto?

"So I see you've decided to continue shooting," Fernando said to Durand, not in a friendly way.

"*Bien sur*...and we safe here...finally," Durand replied, waving his hand at the front door where the APD had blockaded the front entrance.

Fernando shook his head. "You've heard the Hopis...and yet you're still going to steal the Snake Dance."

Durand frowned. "We make art. I tell you that before."

"By trashing their religion? How's that art?"

Durand flipped his wrist, tired of the complaints.

Fernando wasn't about to stop. "What you're doing is sensationalizing the dance—and your movie—to make money. Profit, that's what you make. Nothing but profit."

Shaking his head, Durand and the two men with clipboards hurried off to talk privately, looking back at Fernando, as if wondering what he would do next.

Fernando felt empowered, almost reckless. Durand and the others seemed afraid of him. Wisely none had tried to clobber him with a clipboard like Roberto had done back at Bonanza Creek Ranch. He'd come prepared today, wearing his Smith & Wesson for all the world to see. Let one of them come at him. Just give him a reason. That's all he would need.

Then he spotted Max Russo and Wes Snyder standing over by the wooden ramp. Russo looked worried. He hurried away when he saw Fernando coming toward them. Snyder froze, like a deer in headlights.

"So you killed Roberto," Fernando said to Snyder, as bluntly as possible.

Stunned, Snyder reacted as though he'd been slapped across the face. "You can't prove that."

"Of course I can," Fernando shot back. "I have the note you wrote Roberto asking him to meet you in the La Fonda Parking Garage," he said, another exaggeration. He had no idea what happened to the note. Maybe Manny had it. Anything to make Snyder fear being caught—to make him think the Law was only a step behind him. Some semblance of justice for what he had done.

Snyder started to say something and then stopped. Instead, he turned to follow Russo. He took a couple of steps and then stopped. Turning back to Fernando, he said: "Watch yourself."

Fernando gave him the 'I'm watching you' sign with his hand and then replied, "You too."

READERS GUIDE

1. The mystery begins with Santa Fe photographer Jeff Walker attempting to surreptitiously videotape the Hopi Snake Dance, which is closed to outsiders. How and why does he attempt this?

2. On his way back to Santa Fe Walker is killed when his car runs off a mountain road and falls into a canyon. Is his death an accident—or is it murder?

3. How does former Santa Fe Police Detective Fernando Lopez get involved in all this business—Walker's death and the secret videotape of the Hopi Snake dance?

4. When Lopez helps Walker's wife Gail with her husband's belongings, he finds Walker's iphone and a small camera. What does he do with both devices used to videotape the Snake Dance?

5. Soon after the iphone and camera are recovered, Gail Walker is murder. Who murders her? Why?

6. It turns out that Max Russo's Santa Fe Film Collective and the movie director René Durand (who's currently filming a movie at the Bonanza Creek Ranch south of Santa Fe) both want the secret videotape of the Snake Dance. Explain their reasons for wanting the videotape and their roles in the mystery.

7. Why do Lopez and most Santa Feans object to secretly filming the Hopi Snake Dance and especially to using clips of it in commercial movies? Explain their reasons.

8. Is it, in fact, illegal to film a Native American event closed to outsiders and/or to use that video for commercial purposes? List and explain the possible legal challenges to these uses that Lopez and his colleagues discuss. What do you think?

9. Describe the movie set for 'The Lower World' being filmed by René Durand and his crew at Bonanza Creek Ranch. Why is it so offensive to locals?

10. What finally happens to disrupt and temporarily halt production of 'The Lower World' at Bonanza Creek Ranch? Who's involved?

11. What does René Durand do after the riot at Bonanza Creek Ranch to save the movie? Explain.

12. Lopez admits he partially agrees with Max Russo's cynical description of "end-stage capitalism." What does Russo mean by "end-stage capitalism"? Does the mystery end on this cynical note, or is there reason for hope that violations of Native American culture and religion can be prevented?

THE HOPI SNAKE DANCE
by
D. H. LAWRENCE, 1924

The Hopi country is in Arizona, next the Navajo country, and some seventy miles north of the Santa Fé railroad. The Hopis are Pueblo Indians, village Indians, so their reservation is not large. It consists of a square track of greyish, unappetizing desert, out of which rise three tall arid mesas, broken off in ragged pallid rock. On the top of the mesas perch the ragged, broken, greyish pueblos, identical with the mesas on which they stand.

The nearest village, Walpi, stands in half-ruin high, high on a narrow rock-top where no leaf of life ever was tender. It is all grey, utterly grey, utterly pallid stone and dust, and very narrow. Below it all the stark light of the dry Arizona sun.

Walpi is called the 'first mesa'. And it is at the far edge of Walpi you see the withered beaks and claws and bones of sacrificed eagles, in a rock-cleft under the sky. They sacrifice an eagle each year, on the brink, by rolling him out and crushing him so as to shed no blood. Then they drop his remains down the dry cleft in the promontory's farthest grey tip.

The trail winds on, utterly bumpy and horrible, for thirty miles, past the second mesa, where Chimopova is, on to the third mesa. And on the Sunday afternoon of 17th August black automobile after automobile lurched and crawled across the grey desert, where low, grey, sage-scrub was coming to pallid yellow. Black hood followed crawling after black hood, like a funeral cortège. The motor-cars, with all the tourists wending their way to the third and farthest mesa, thirty miles across this dismal desert where an odd water-windmill spun, and odd patches of corn blew in the strong desert wind, like dark-green women with fringed shawls blowing and fluttering, not far from the foot of the great, grey, up-piled mesa.

The snake dance (I am told) is held once a year, on each of the three mesas in succession. This year of grace 1924 it was to be held in Hotevilla, the last village on the farthest western tip of the third mesa.

On and on bumped the cars. The lonely second mesa lay in the distance. On and on, to the ragged ghost of the third mesa.

The third mesa has two main villages, Oraibi, which is on the near edge, and Hotevilla, on the far. Up scrambles the car, on all its four legs, like a black-beetle straddling past the school-house and store down below, up the bare rock and over the changeless boulders, with a surge and a sickening lurch to the sky-brim, where stands the rather foolish church. Just beyond, dry, grey, ruined, and apparently abandoned, Oraibi, its few ragged stone huts. All these cars come all this way, and apparently nobody at home.

You climb still, up the shoulder of rock, a few more miles, across the lofty, wind-swept mesa, and so you come to Hote-villa, where the dance is, and where already hundreds of motor-cars are herded in an official camping-ground, among the piñon bushes.

Hotevilla is a tiny little village of grey little houses, raggedly built with undressed stone and mud around a little oblong *plaza*, and partly in ruins. One of the chief two-storey houses on the small square is a ruin, with big square window-holes.

It is a parched, grey country of snakes and eagles, pitched up against the sky. And a few dark-faced, short, thickly built Indians have their few peach trees among the sand, their beans and squashes on the naked sand under the sky, their springs of brackish water.

Three thousand people came to see the little snake dance this year, over miles of desert and bumps. Three thousand, of all sorts, cultured people from New York, Californians, onward-pressing tourists, cowboys, Navajo Indians, even Negroes; fathers, mothers, children, of all ages, colours, sizes of stoutness, dimensions of curiosity.

What had they come for? Mostly to see men hold *live rattlesnakes* in their mouths. '*I never did see a rattlesnake and I'm crazy to see one!*' cried a girl with bobbed hair.

There you have it. People trail hundreds of miles, avidly, to see this circus-performance of men handling live rattlesnakes that may bite them any minute–even do bite them. Some show, that!

There is the other aspect, of the ritual dance. One may look on from the angle of culture, as one looks on while Anna Pavlova dances with the Russian Ballet.

Or there is still another point of view, the religious. Before the snake dance begins, on the Monday, and the spectators are packed thick on the ground round the square, and in the window-holes, and on all the roofs, all sorts of people greedy with curiosity, a little speech is made to them all, asking the audience to be silent and respectful, as this is a sacred religious ceremonial of the Hopi Indians, and not a public entertainment. Therefore, please, no clapping or cheering or applause, but remember you are, as it were, in a church.

The audience accepts the implied rebuke in good faith, and looks round with a grin at the 'church'. But it is a good-humoured, very decent crowd, ready to respect any sort of feelings. And the Indian with his 'religion' is a sort of public pet.

From the cultured point of view, the Hopi snake dance is almost nothing, not much more than a circus turn, or the games that children play in the street. It has none of the impressive beauty of the Corn Dance at Santo Domingo, for example. The big pueblos of Zuni, Santo Domingo, Taos have a cultured instinct which is not revealed in the Hopi snake dance. This last is uncouth rather than beautiful, and rather uncouth in its touch of horror. Hence the thrill, and the crowd.

As a cultured spectacle, it is a circus turn: men actually dancing round with snakes, poisonous snakes, dangling from their mouths.

And as a religious ceremonial: well, you can either be politely tolerant like the crowd to the Hopis; or you must have some spark of understanding of the sort of religion implied.

'Oh, the Indians,' I heard a woman say, they believe we are all brothers, the snakes are the Indians' brothers, and the Indians are the snakes' brothers. The Indians would never hurt the snakes, they won't hurt any animal. So the snakes won't bite the Indians. They are all brothers, and none of them hurt anybody.'

This sounds very nice, only more Hindoo than Hopi. The dance itself does not convey much sense of fraternal communion. It is not in the least like St Francis preaching to the birds.

The animistic religion, as we call it, is not the religion of the Spirit. A religion of spirits, yes. But not of Spirit. There is no One Spirit. There is no One God. There is no Creator. There is strictly no God at all: because all is alive. In our conception of religion there exists God and His Creation: two things. We are creatures of God, therefore we pray to God as the Father, the Saviour, the Maker.

But strictly, in the religion of aboriginal America, there is no Father, and no Maker. There is the great living source of life: say the Sun of existence: to which you can no more pray than you can pray to Electricity. And emerging from this Sun are the great potencies, the invincible influences which make shine and warmth and rain. From these great interrelated potencies of rain and heat and thunder emerge the seeds of life itself, corn, and creatures like snakes. And beyond these, men, persons. But all emerge separately. There is no oneness, no sympathetic identifying oneself with the rest. The law of isolation is heavy on every creature.

Now the Sun, the rain, the shine, the thunder, they are alive. But they are not persons or people. They are alive. They are manifestations of living activity. But they are not personal Gods.

Everything lives. Thunder lives, and rain lives, and sunshine lives. But not in the personal sense.

How is man to get himself into relation with the vast living convulsions of rain and thunder and sun, which are conscious and alive and potent, but like vastest of beasts, inscrutable and incomprehensible. How is man to get himself into relation with these, the vastest of cosmic beasts?

It is the problem of the ages of man. Our religion says the cosmos is Matter, to be conquered by the Spirit of Man. The yogi, the fakir, the saint try conquest by abnegation and by psychic powers. The real conquest of the cosmos is made by science.

The American-Indian sees no division into Spirit and Matter, God and not-God. Everything is alive, though not personally so. Thunder is neither Thor nor Zeus. Thunder is the vast living thunder asserting itself like some incomprehensible monster, or some huge reptile-bird of the pristine cosmos.

How to conquer the dragon-mouthed thunder! How to capture the feathered rain!

We make reservoirs, and irrigation ditches and artesian wells. We make lightning conductors, and build vast electric plants. We say it is a matter of science, energy, force.

But the Indian says No! It all lives. We must approach it fairly, with profound respect, but also with desperate courage. Because man must conquer the cosmic monsters of living thunder and live rain. The rain that slides down from its source, and ebbs back subtly, with a strange energy generated between its coming and going, an energy which, even to our science, is of life: this, man has to conquer. The serpent-striped, feathery Rain.

We made the conquest by dams and reservoirs and windmills. The Indian, like the old Egyptian, seeks to make the conquest from the mystic will within him, pitted against the Cosmic Dragon.

We must remember, to the animistic vision there is no perfect God behind us, who created us from his knowledge, and foreordained all things. No such God. Behind lies only the terrific, terrible, crude Source, the mystic Sun, the well-head of all things. From this mystic Sun emanate the Dragons, Rain, Wind, Thunder Shine, Light. The Potencies of Powers. These bring forth Earth, then reptiles, birds, and fishes.

The Potencies are not Gods. They are Dragons. The Sun of Creation itself is a dragon most terrible, vast, and most powerful, yet even so, less in being than we. The only gods on earth are men. For gods, like man, do not exist beforehand. They are created and evolved gradually, with aeons of effort, out of the fire and smelting of life. They are the highest thing created, smelted between the furnace of the Life-Sun, and beaten on the anvil of the rain, with hammers or thunder and bellows of rushing wind. The cosmos is a great furnace, a dragon's den, where the heroes and demi-gods, men, forge themselves into being. It is a vast and violent matrix, where souls form like diamonds in earth, under extreme pressure.

So that gods are the outcome, not the origin. And the best gods that have resulted, so far, are men. But gods frail as flowers; which have also the godliness of things that have won perfection out of the terrific dragon-clutch of the cosmos. Men are frail as flowers. Man is as a flower, rain can kill him or succour him, heat can flick him with a bright tail, and destroy him: or, on the other hand, it can softly call him into existence, out of the egg of chaos. Man is delicate as a flower, godly beyond flowers, and his lordship is a ticklish business.

He has to conquer, and hold his own, and again conquer all the time. Conquer the powers of the cosmos. To us, science is our religion of conquest. Hence through science, we are the conquerors and resultant gods of our earth. But to the Indian, the so-called mechanical processes do not exist. All lives. And the conquest is made by the means of the living will.

This is the religion of all aboriginal America. Peruvian, Aztec, Athabascan: perhaps the aboriginal religion of all the word. In Mexico, men fell into horror of the crude, pristine gods, the dragons. But to the pueblo Indian, the most terrible dragon is still somewhat gentle-hearted.

This brings us back to the Hopi. He has the hardest task, the stubbornest destiny. Some inward fate drove him to the top of these parched mesas, all rocks and eagles, sand and snakes, and wind and sun and alkali. These he had to conquer. Not merely, as we should put it, the natural conditions of the place. But the mysterious life-spirit that reigned there. The eagle and the snake.

It is a destiny as well as another. The destiny of the animistic soul of man, instead of our destiny of Mind and Spirit. We have undertaken the scientific conquest of forces, of natural conditions. It has been comparatively easy, and we are victors. Look at our black motor-cars like beetles working up the rock-face at Oraibi. Look at our three thousand tourists gathered to gaze at the twenty lonely men who dance in the tribe's snake dance!

The Hopi sought the conquest by means of the mystic, living will that is in man, pitted against the living will of the dragon-cosmos. The Egyptians long ago made a partial conquest by the same means. We have made a partial conquest by other means. Our corn doesn't fail us: we have no seven years' famine, and apparently need never have. But the other thing fails us, the strange inward sun of life; the pellucid monster of the rain never shows us his stripes. To us, heaven switches on daylight, or turns on the shower-bath. We little gods are gods of the machine only. It is our highest. Our cosmos is a great *ennui*. And we die of ennui. A subtle dragon stings us in the midst of plenty. *Quos vult perdere Deus, dementat prius.*

On the Sunday evening is a first little dance in the plaza at Hotevilla, called the Antelope dance. There is the hot, sandy, oblong little place, with a tuft of green cotton-wood boughs stuck like a plume at the south end, and on the floor at the foot of the green, a little lid of a trap-door. They say the snakes are under there.

They say that the twelve officiating men of the snake clan of the tribe have for nine days been hunting snakes in the rocks. They have been performing the mysteries for nine days, in the kiva, and for two days they have fasted completely. All these days they have tended the snakes, washed them with repeated lustrations, soothed them, and exchanged spirits with them. The spirit of man soothing and seeking and making interchange with the spirits of the snakes. For the snakes are more rudimentary, nearer to the great convulsive powers. Nearer to the nameless Sun, more knowing in the slanting tracks of the rain, the pattering of the invisible feet of the rain-monster from the sky. The snakes are man's next emissaries to the rain-gods. The snakes lie nearer to the source of potency, the dark, lurking, intense sun at the center of the earth. For to the cultured animist, and the pueblo Indian is such, the earth's dark center holds its dark sun, our source of isolated being, round which our world coils its folds like a great snake. The snake is nearer the dark sun, and cunning of it.

They say–people say–that rattlesnakes are not travelers. They haunt the same spots on earth, and die there. It is said also that the snake priest (so-called) of the Hopi probably capture the same snakes year after year.

Be that as it may. At sundown before the real dance, there is the little dance called the Antelope Dance. We stand and wait on a house-roof. Behind us is tethered an eagle; rather dishevelled he sits on the coping, and looks at us in unutterable resentment. See him, and see how much 'brotherhood' the Indian feels with animals–at best the silent tolerance that acknowledges dangerous difference. We wait without event. There are no drums, no announcements. Suddenly into the *plaza*, with rude, intense movements, hurried a little file of men. They are smeared all with grey and black, and are naked save for little kilts embroidered like the sacred dance-kilts in other pueblos, red and green and black on a white fibre-cloth. The fox-skins hangs behind. The feet of the dancers are pure ash-grey. Their hair is long.

The first is a heavy old man with heavy, long, wild grey hair and heavy fringe. He plods intensely forward in the silence, followed in a sort of circle by the other grey-smeared, longhaired, naked, concentrated men. The oldest men are first: the last is a short-haired boy of fourteen or fifteen. There are only eight men–the so-called antelope priests. They pace round in a circle, rudely, absorbedly, till the first heavy, intense old man with his massive grey hair flowing, comes to the lid on the ground, near the tuft of kiva-boughs. He rapidly shakes from the hollow of his right hand a little white meal on the lid, stamps heavily, with naked right foot, on the meal, so the wood resounds, and paces heavily forward. Each man, to the boy, shakes meal, stamps, paces absorbedly on in the circle, comes to the lid again, shakes meal, stamps, paces absorbedly on, comes a third time to the lid, or trap-door, and this time spits on the lid, stamps, and goes on. And this time the eight men file away behind the lid, between it and the tuft of green boughs. And there they stand in a line, their backs to the kivatuft of green; silent, absorbed, bowing a little to the ground.

Suddenly paces with rude haste another file of men. They are naked, and smeared with red 'medicine', with big black lozenges of smeared paint on their backs. Their wild heavy hair hangs loose, the old, heavy, grey-haired men go first, then the middle-aged, then the young men, then last, two short-haired, slim boys, schoolboys. The hair of the young men, growing after school, is bobbed round.

The grown men are all heavily built, rather short, with heavy but shapely flesh, and rather straight sides. They have not the archaic slim waists of the Taos Indians. They have archaic squareness, and a sensuous heaviness. Their very hair is black, massive, heavy. These are the so-called snake-priests, men of the snake clan. And tonight they are eleven in number.

They pace rapidly round, with that heavy wild silence of concentration characteristic of them, and cast meal and stamp upon the lid, cast meal and stamp in the second round, come round and spit and stamp in the third. For to the savage, the animist, to spit may be a kind of blessing, a communion, a sort of embrace.

The eleven snake-priests form silently in a row, facing the eight grey smeared antelope-priests across the little lid, and bowing forward a little, to earth. Then the antelope-priests, bending forward, begin a low, sombre chant, or call, that sounds wordless, only a deep, low-toned, secret Ay-a! Ay-a! Ay-a! And they bend from right to left, giving two shakes to the little, flat, white rattle in their left hand, at each shake, and stamping the right foot in heavy rhythm. In their right hand, that held the meal, is grasped a little skin bag, perhaps also containing meal.

They lean from right to left, two seed-like shakes of the rattle each time and the heavy rhythmic stamp of the foot, and the low, sombre, secretive chant-call each time. It is a strange low sound, such as we never hear, and it reveals how deep, how deep the men are in the mystery they are practising, how sunk deep below our world, to the world of snakes, and dark ways in the earth, where the roots of corn, and where the little rivers of unchannelled, uncreated life-passion run like dark, trickling lightning, to the roots of the corn and to the feet and loins of men, from the earth's innermost dark sun. They are calling in the deep, almost silent snake-language, to the snakes and the rays of dark emission from the earth's inward 'Sun'.

At this moment, a silence falls on the whole crowd of listeners. It is that famous darkness and silence of Egypt, the touch of the other mystery. The deep concentration of the 'priests' conquers for a few seconds our white-faced flippancy, and we hear only the deep Hah-hà! Hah-ha! speaking to snakes and the earth's inner core.

This lasts a minute or two. Then the antelope-priests stand bowed and still, and the snake-priests take up the swaying and the deep chant, that sometimes is so low, it is like a mutter underground, inaudible. The rhythm is crude, the swaying unison is all uneven. Culturally, there is nothing. If it were not for that mystic, dark-sacred concentration.

Several times in turn, the two rows of daubed, long-haired, insunk men facing one another take up the swaying and the chant. Then that too is finished. There is a break in the formation. A young snake-priest takes up something that may be a corn-cob–perhaps an antelope-priest hands it to him–and comes forward, with an old, heavy, but still shapely snake-priest behind him dusting his shoulders with the feathers, eagle-feathers presumably, which are the Indians' hollow prayer-sticks. With the heavy, stamping hop they move round in the previous circle, the young priest holding the cob curiously, and the old priest prancing strangely at the young priest's hack, in a sort of incantation, and brushing the heavy young shoulders delicately with the prayer-feathers. It is the God-vibration that enters us from behind, and is transmitted to the hands, from the hands to the corn-cob. Several young priests emerge, with the bowed heads and the cob in their hands and the heavy older priests hanging over them behind. They tread round the rough curve and come back to the kiva, take perhaps another cob, and tread round again.

That is all. In ten or fifteen minutes it is over. The two files file rapidly and silently away. A brief, primitive performance.

The crowd disperses. They were not many people. There were no venomous snakes on exhibition, so the mass had nothing to come for. And therefore the curious immersed intensity of the priests was able to conquer the white crowd.

By afternoon of the next day the three thousand people had massed in the little *plaza*, secured themselves places on the roof and in the window-spaces, everywhere, till the small pueblo seemed built of people instead of stones. All sorts of people, hundreds and hundreds of white women, all in breeches like half-men, hundreds and hundreds of men who had been driving motor-cars, then many Navajos, the women in their full, long skirts and tight velvet bodices, the men rather lanky, long-waisted, real nomads. In the hot sun and the wind which blows the sand every day, every day in volumes round the corners, the three thousand tourists sat for hours, waiting for the show. The Indian policeman cleared the central oblong, in front of the kiva. The front rows of onlookers sat thick on the ground. And at last, rather early, because of the masses awaiting them, suddenly, silently, in the same rude haste, the antelope-priests filed absorbedly in, and made the rounds over the lid, as before. Today, the eight antelope-priests were very grey. Their feet ashed pure grey, like suède soft boots: and their lower jaw was pure suède grey, while the rest of their face was blackish. With that pale-grey jaw, they looked like corpse-faces with swathing-bands. And all their bodies ash-grey smeared, with smears of black, and a black cloth today at the loins.

They made their rounds, and took their silent position behind the lid, with backs to the green tuft: an unearthly grey row of men with little skin bags in their hands. They were the lords of shadow, the intermediate twilight, the place of afterlife and before-life, where house the winds of change. Lords of the mysterious, fleeting power of change.

Suddenly, with abrupt silence, in paced the snake-priests, headed by the same heavy man with solid grey hair like iron. Today they were twelve men, from the old one, down to the slight, short-haired, erect boy of fourteen. Twelve men, two for each of the six worlds, or quarters: east, north, south, west, above, and below. And today they were in a queer ecstasy. Their faces were black, showing the whites of the eyes. And they wore small black loin-aprons. They were the hot living men of the darkness, lords of the earth's inner rays, the black sun of the earth's vital core, from which dart the speckled snakes, like beams.

Round they went, in rapid, uneven, silent absorption, the three rounds. Then in a row they faced the eight ash-grey men, across the lid. All kept their heads bowed towards earth, except the young boys.

Then, in the intense, secret, muttering chant the grey men began their leaning from right to left, shaking the hand, one-two, one-two, and bowing the body each time from right to left, left to right, above the lid in the ground, under which were the snakes. And their low, deep, mysterious voices spoke to the spirits under the earth, not to men above the earth.

But the crowd was on tenterhooks for the snakes, and could hardly wait for the mummery to cease. There was an atmosphere of inattention and impatience. But the chant and the swaying passed from the grey men to the black-faced men, and back again, several times.

This was finished. The formation of the lines broke up. There was a slight crowding to the centre, round the lid. The old antelope-priest (so called) was stooping. And before the crowd could realize anything else a young priest emerged, bowing reverently, with the neck of a pale, delicate rattlesnake held between his teeth, the little, naïve, bird-like head of the rattlesnake quite still, near the black cheek, and the long, pale, yellowish, spangled body of the snake dangling like some thick, beautiful cord. On passed the black-faced young priest, with the wondering snake dangling from his mouth, pacing in the original circle, while behind him, leaping almost on his shoulders, was the oldest heavy priest, dusting the young man's shoulders with the feather-prayer-sticks, in an intense, earnest anxiety of concentration such as I have only seen in the old Indian men during a religious dance.

Came another young black-faced man out of the confusion, with another snake dangling and writhing a little from his mouth, and an elder priest dusting him from behind with the feathers: and then another, and another: till it was all confusion, probably, of six, and then four young priests with snakes dangling from their mouths, going round, apparently, three times in the circle. At the end of the third round the young priest stooped and delicately laid his snake on the earth, waving him away, away, as it were, into the world. He must not wriggle back to the kiva bush.

And after wondering a moment, the pale, delicate snake steered away with a rattlesnake's beautiful movement, rippling and looping, with the small, sensitive head lifted like antennae, across the sand to the massed audience squatting solid on the ground around. Like soft, watery lightning went the wondering snake at the crowd. As he came nearer, the people began to shrink aside, half-mesmerized. But they betrayed no exaggerated fear. And as the little snake drew very near, up rushed one of the two black-faced young priests who held the snake-stick, poised a moment over the snake, in the prayer-concentration of reverence which is at the same time conquest, and snatched the pale, long creature delicately from the ground, waving him in a swoop over the heads of the seated crowd, then delicately smoothing down the length of the snake with his left hand, stroking and smoothing and soothing the long, pale, bird-like thing; and returning with it to the kiva, handed it to one of the grey-jawed antelope-priests.

Meanwhile, all the time, the other young priests were emerging with a snake dangling from their mouths. The boy had finished his rounds. He launched his rattlesnake on the ground, like a ship, and like a ship away it steered. In a moment, after it went one of those two black-faced priests who carried snake-sticks and were the snake-catchers. As it neared the crowd, very close, he caught it up and waved it dramatically, his eyes glaring strangely out of his black face. And in the interim that youngest boy had been given a long, handsome bull-snake, by the priest at the hole under the kiva boughs. The bull-snake is not poisonous. It is a constrictor. This one was six feet long, with a sumptuous pattern. It waved its pale belly, and pulled its neck out of the boy's mouth. With two hands he put it back. It pulled itself once more free. Again he got it back, and managed to hold it. And then as he went round in his looping circle, it coiled its handsome folds twice round his knee. He stooped, quietly, and as quietly as if he were untying his garter, he unloosed the folds. And all the time, an old priest was intently brushing the boy's thin straight shoulders with the feathers. And all the time, the snakes seemed strangely gentle, naïve, wondering and almost willing, almost in harmony with the man. Which of course was the sacred aim. While the boy's expression remained quite still and simple, as it were candid, in a candour where he and the snake should be in unison. The only dancers who showed signs of being wrought-up were the two young snake-catchers, and one of these, particularly, seemed in a state of actor-like uplift, rather ostentatious. But the old priests had that immersed, religious intentness which is like a spell, something from another world.

The young boy launched his bull-snake. It wanted to go back to the kiva. The snake-catcher drove it gently forward. Away it went, towards the crowd, and at the last minute was caught up into the air. Then this snake was handed to an old man sitting on the ground in the audience, in the front row. He was an old Hopi of the Snake clan.

Snake after snake had been carried round in the circles, dangling by the neck from the mouths of one young priest or another, and writhing and swaying slowly, with the small, delicate snake-head held as if wondering and listening. There had been some very large rattlesnakes, unusually large, two or three handsome bull-snakes, and some racers, whipsnakes. All had been launched, after their circuits in the mouth, all had been caught up by the young priests with the snake-sticks, one or two had been handed to old-snake clan men in the audience, who sat holding them in their arms as men hold a kitten. The most of the snakes, however, had been handed to the grey antelope-men who stood in the row with their backs to the kiva bush. Till some of these ash-smeared men held armfuls of snakes, hanging over their arms like wet washing. Some of the snakes twisted and knotted round one another, showing pale bellies.

Yet most of them hung very still and docile. Docile, almost sympathetic, so that one was struck only by their clean, slim length of snake nudity, their beauty, like soft, quiescent lightning. They were so clean, because they had been washed and anointed and lustrated by the priests, in the days they had been in the kiva.

At last all the snakes had been mouth-carried in the circuits, and had made their little outrunning excursion to the crowd, and had been handed back to the priests in the rear. And now the Indian policemen, Hopi and Navajo, began to clear away the crowd that sat on the ground, five or six rows deep, around the small *plaza*. The snakes were all going to be set free on the ground. We must clear away.

We recoiled to the farther end of the *plaza*. There, two Hopi women were scattering white corn-meal on the sandy ground. And thither came the two snake-catchers, almost at once, with their arms full of snakes. And before we who stood had realized it, the snakes were all writhing and squirming on the ground, in the white dust of meal, a couple of yards from our feet. Then immediately, before they could writhe clear of each other and steer away, they were gently, swiftly snatched up again, and with their arms full of snakes, the two young priests went running out of the *plaza*.

We followed slowly, wondering, towards the western, or north-western edge of the mesa. There the mesa dropped steeply, and a broad trail wound down to the vast hollow of desert brimmed up with strong evening light, up out of which jutted a perspective of sharp rock and further mesas and distant sharp mountains: the great, hollow, rock-wilderness space of that part of Arizona, submerged in light.

Away down the trail, small, dark, naked, rapid figures with arms held close, went the two young men, running swiftly down to the hollow level, and diminishing, running across the hollow towards more stark rocks of the other side. Two small, rapid, intent, dwindling little human figures. The tiny, dark sparks of men. Such specks of gods.

They disappeared, no bigger than stones, behind rocks in shadow. They had gone, it was said, to lay down the snakes before a rock called the snake-shrine, and let them all go free. Free to carry the message and thanks to the dragon-gods who can give and withhold. To carry the human spirit, the human breath, the human prayer, the human gratitude, the human command which had been breathed upon them in the mouths of the priests, transferred into them from those feather-prayersticks which the old wise men swept upon the shoulders of the young, snake-bearing men, to carry this back, into the vaster, dimmer, inchoate regions where the monsters of rain and wind alternated in beneficence and wrath. Carry the human prayer and will-power into the holes of the winds, down into the octopus heart of the rain-source. Carry the corn-meal which the women had scattered, back to that terrific, dread, and causeful dark sun which is at the earth's core, that which sends us corn out of the earth's nearness, sends us food or death, according to our strength of vital purpose, our power of sensitive will, our courage.

It is a battle, a wrestling all the time. The Sun, the nameless Sun, source of all things, which we call sun because the other name is too fearful, this, this vast dark protoplasmic sun from which issues all that feeds our life, this original One is all the time willing and unwilling. Systole, diastole, it pulses its willingness and its unwillingness that we should live and move on, from being to being, manhood to further manhood. Man, small, vulnerable man, the farthest adventurer from the dark heart of the first of suns, into the cosmos of creation. Man, the last god won into existence. And all the time, he is sustained and threated, menaced and sustained from the Source, the innermost sun-dragon. And all the time, he must submit and he must conquer. Submit to the strange beneficence from the Source, whose ways are past finding out. And conquer the strange malevolence of the Source, which is past comprehension also.

For the great dragons from which we draw our vitality are all the time willing and unwilling that we should have being. Hence only the heroes snatch manhood, little by little, from the strange den of the Cosmos.

Man, little man, with his consciousness and his will, must both submit to the great origin- powers of his life, and conquer them. Conquered by man who has overcome his fears, the snakes must go back into the earth with his messages of tenderness, of request, and of power. They go back as rays of love to the dark heart of the first of suns. But they go back also as arrows shot clean by man's sapience and courage, into the resistant, malevolent heart of the earth's oldest, stubborn core. In the core of the first of suns, whence man draws his vitality, lies poison as bitter as the rattlesnake's. This poison man must overcome, he must be master of its issue. Because from the first of suns come travelling the rays that make men strong and glad and gods who can range between the known and the unknown. Rays that quiver out of the earth as serpents do, naked with vitality. But each ray charged with poison for the unwary, the irreverent, and the cowardly. Awareness, wariness, is the first virtue in primitive man's morality. And his awareness must travel back and forth, back and forth, from the darkest origins out to the brightest edifices of creation.

And amid all its crudity, and the sensationalism which comes chiefly out of the crowd's desire for thrills, one cannot help pausing in reverence before the delicate, anointed bravery of the snake-priests (so called), with the snakes.

They say the Hopis have a marvelous secret cure for snakebites. They say the bitten are given an emetic drink, after the dance, by the old women, and that they must lie on the edge of the cliff and vomit, vomit, vomit. I saw none of this. The two snake-men who ran down into the shadow came soon running up again, running all the while, and steering off at a tangent, ran up the mesa once more, but beyond a deep, impassable cleft. And there, when they had come up to our level, we saw them across the cleft distance washing, brown and naked, in a pool; washing off the paint, the medicine, the ecstasy, to come back into daily life and eat food. Because for two days they had eaten nothing, it was said. And for nine days they had been immersed in the mystery of snakes, and fasting in some measure.

Men who have lived many years among the Indians say they do not believe the Hopi have any secret cure. Sometimes priests do die of bites, it is said. But a rattlesnake secretes his poison slowly. Each time he strikes he loses his venom, until if he strikes several times, he has very little wherewithal to poison a man. Not enough, not half enough to kill. His glands must be very full charged with poison, as they are when he emerges from winter-sleep, before he can kill a man outright. And even then, he must strike near some artery.

Therefore, during the nine days of the kiva, when the snakes are bathed and lustrated, perhaps they strike their poison away into some inanimate object. And surely they are soothed and calmed with such things as the priests, after centuries of experience, know how to administer to them.

We dam the Nile and take the railway across America. The Hopi smooths the rattlesnake and carries him in his mouth, to send him back into the dark places of the earth, an emissary to the inner powers.

To each sort of man his own achievement, his own victory, his own conquest. To the Hopi, the origins are dark and dual, cruelty is coiled in the very beginnings of all things, and circle after circle creation emerges towards a flickering, revealed Godhead. With Man as the godhead so far achieved, waveringly and forever incomplete, in this world.

To us and to the Orientals, the Godhead was perfect to start with, and man makes but a mechanical excursion into a created and ordained universe, an excursion of mechanical achievement, and of yearning for the return to the perfect Godhead of the beginning.

To us, God was in the beginning, Paradise and the Golden Age have been long lost, and all we can do is to win back.

To the Hopi, God is not yet, and the Golden Age lies far ahead. Out of the dragon's den of the cosmos, we have wrested only the beginnings of our being, the rudiments of our Godhead.

Between the two visions lies the gulf of mutual negations. But ours was the quickest way, so we are conquerors for the moment.

The American aborigines are radically, innately religious. The fabric of their life is religion. But their religion is animistic, their sources are dark and impersonal, their conflict with their 'gods' is slow, and unceasing.

This is true of the settled pueblo Indian and the wandering Navajo, the ancient Maya, and the surviving Aztec. They are all involved at every moment, in their old, struggling religion.

Until they break in a kind of hopelessness under our cheerful, triumphant success. Which is what is rapidly happening. The young Indians who have been to school for many years are losing their religion, becoming discontented, bored, and rootless. An Indian with his own religion inside him *cannot* be bored. The flow of the mystery is too intense all the time, too intense, even, for him to adjust himself to circumstances which really are mechanical. Hence his failure. So he, in his great religious struggle for the Godhead of man, falls back beaten. The Personal God who ordained a mechanical cosmos gave the victory to his sons, a mechanical triumph.

Soon after the dance is over, the Navajo begin to ride down the Western trail, into the light. Their women, with velvet bodices and full, full skirts, silver and turquoise tinkling thick on their breasts, sit back on their horses and ride down the steep slope, looking wonderingly around from their pleasant, broad, nomadic, Mongolian faces. And the men, long, loose, thin, long-waisted, with tall hats on their brows and low-sunk silver belts on their hips, come down to water their horses at the spring. We say they look wild. But they have the remoteness of their religion, their animistic vision, in their eyes, they can't see as we see. And they cannot accept us. They stare at us as the coyotes stare at us: the gulf of mutual negation between us.

So in groups, in pairs, singly, they ride silently down into the lower strata of light, the aboriginal Americans riding into their shut-in reservations. While the white Americans hurry back to their motor-cars, and soon the air buzzes with starting engines, like the biggest of rattlesnakes buzzing.